THIEF OF DREAMS

BEC MCMASTER

Lochaber
PRESS

THIEF OF DREAMS

When Prince Keir of the Court of Dreams sends out a summons in search of a bride, the Wraith King sees a chance to steal the powerful Dragon's Heart. He sends his best thief, Zemira Az Ghul, to penetrate the court as one of the potential brides.

All Zemira wants is freedom from the chains that bind her to the king, and if she finds the relic she'll have it. But the Court of Dreams is more dangerous than she ever expected, and Zemira must soon choose between her freedom—and her heart.

1

The Wraith King sits on his throne, ghostly pale hands resting on the arms as I enter the audience chamber, my heeled boots clicking on the polished obsidian tiles. I briefly consider telling him the flickering sconces and smattering of winter-scoured skulls are precisely why the gilded fae courts consider those of my kind abominations, but I like my tongue where it is, thank you very much.

Raesh Ghul, the Wraith King Beyond the Shadowfangs.

Master of Bone and Death.

The creature that holds my fate in his clawed hands.

A crown carved from a troll's skull rests on his long, raven-black hair, and those bottomless eyes lock on me with an eerie intensity. Intimidating, to say the least. A pale wolf pelt rests over his bare shoulders, a golden chain around his throat dripping with tiny glass vials. Wisps of insubstantial light fill them, an almost hypnotic glow. Subtle, he is not.

And capturing his attention is never wise.

But nobody ever called me wise before.

"You sent for me, Father?" I ask, trying to stop my gaze

from sliding to those glowing glass vials. Especially the one in the center, where a tendril of glowing white light senses my presence and reaches out to press itself against the glass.

I yearn for it too. Yearn to be whole again.

"You're late."

"I was training," I reply. "Forgive me for not anticipating your desire to see me. It seems the messenger was waylaid."

"Your sister managed to arrive on time."

What a surprise. "One of her many attributes."

I pause below the dais, next to the kneeling supplicant already waiting there. Black silk flows from her shoulders and her shining black hair is woven into a dozen braids as she keeps her head bowed. Once upon a time, we were reflections in a mirror, but Soraya no longer has an interest in being the other half of me.

And for some reason, she didn't want Father's messenger to reach me.

"I see no need to delay further on pleasantries. I have a job for my thief."

"I can do it, Father," Soraya says, looking up from her kneeling position. "Let *me* do it."

This captures my interest. There's no love lost between my sister and me, but she has her gifts. I have mine. While Soraya can stop a man's heart with a single smile, I can pluck the last coin from a miser's purse while he's watching it.

She must still be smarting from that failed assassination attempt last month.

"This job is delicate. It requires the best," Raesh replies. "I've spent three thousand years waiting for this chance, and I will not see it slip through my fingers." He leans forward hungrily. "A single failure means we will never get such a chance again."

Three thousand years?

"You want me to steal from one of the fae." Of the long-lived races, they're the only ones who've been around that long—and survived.

It wouldn't be the first time I slipped among the lighter courts. After all, it's why I was created; a half-fae, half-wraith creature that can pass as either, though my features throw more toward my mother's people than my father's.

Thank the moon.

My father's ghostly pallor would not go well with the simple black velvet doublet I wear. It wouldn't go well with anything.

Except perhaps a coffin.

Perhaps that's why he likes his bleached skulls so much?

"Not just *one* of the fae," Soraya interrupts angrily. "You're asking her to pull the wool over the eyes of a ruling prince. Zemira's shown her weakness in the past. *I* am the best. *I* was your Champion. Her heart is too soft."

And yours made of solid stone. If you ever had one.

But that's neither here nor there.

"What's the job? Which ruling prince?" I ask. There are over two dozen fae courts, each lovelier and more dangerous than the one before it, but fae males rule only a handful. "Court of Shadows? Court of Blood? Court of Storms?"

Fingers crossing behind my back, I hope and pray it's not the Court of Storms.

Prince Angmar still resents me for the loss of his trident. Each court's power is focused through a relic of some description that is tied to the ruling prince or queen, and there are whispers his manhood wanes without it. I'm told my head is worth its weight in gold to him, and I much prefer it where it is.

Those black eyes lock on me again. "I want you to steal the Dragon's Heart from Prince Keir's Court of Dreams."

And now the floor drops out from under me. "Are you *insane?*"

Breaking into the Court of Dreams is a death trap.

There's only one way in and out—a heavily guarded portal—and nobody knows where the portal leads. Nobody knows where the Court of Dreams even resides. Some whisper of an Other World, created by the dreams of dragons long ago, but nobody actually knows. It's not located on any of the continents I know of. It may not even exist.

Just a tale woven of myth and shadow.

"Some say there is no Court of Dreams," I protest. "That it was lost to memory, and that—"

"It exists," Raesh snarls, his claws digging into the arms of the throne. "Though Keir tore it from the mortal world long ago, and its only been seen rarely ever since. There is rumor the portal is waking."

"I'd be working blind," I blurt. "There's no schematics, no information about the Dragon's Heart or where he hides it.... Nobody's even crossed the portal into the Court of Dreams in—"

"Three thousand years," Soraya mutters.

I shake my head. "It can't be done. My magic works perfectly to help me slip about unseen in fae palaces, but I can't cross the portal without Keir—or one of his guards—knowing. I can't even activate the portal without his say-so. You're asking for the impossible. The Court of Dreams is dangerous."

And then, of course, there's the Prince of Dreams himself.

He alone stood apart during the Dragon Wars all those

years ago. He faced the combined might of the fae courts when he wouldn't agree to their terms, and when they threatened him with annihilation, he simply tore his court from the mortal plane and vanished it.

"No, you cannot cross the portal without Keir knowing. Unless, of course, the portal is open and you have an invitation," Raesh purrs. He looks entirely too pleased with himself.

"I must have misplaced it," I drawl, heart still pounding.

"Not you, specifically. Keir's sent out a Summons."

A Summons.

A bride hunt.

Every fae princess in the land will be waiting with bated breath for that invitation. Keir's may be a name whispered in hushed tones in case he overhears, but he's incredibly powerful. A living legend. Rich. Dominant. The ultimate catch for any female with breath in her lungs.

Good luck to the poor soul who lands him.

But it might be a way in.

I hold up my arms, releasing my grip on the glamour that keeps my true nature under wraps. A faint, unearthly luminescence begins to glow beneath my skin. Without glancing at my reflection in the polished obsidian floors, I know my eyes have become completely black, the thin tracery of blackened capillaries lacing through my cheeks, and my hair gleams like silver under moonlight. "Somehow I doubt the Prince of Dreams thought to include one of the Forbidden on his potential bride list. Wouldn't want to taint his precious blood."

"No." Raesh tosses me a scroll. "But here's a list of those females that *have* been granted such an invitation."

There are nearly two dozen names on the list.

And suddenly I know what he's suggesting.

All I need is an invitation and a name not my own.

None of the princesses of the Blessed Courts, for they're too well known. But there are the names of more obscure titles here. Lady of the Golden Dawn. Duchess of Goldenrod. Lady of Greenslieves.

Nobody would miss any of them.

And there's a fair chance no one has *seen* any of them.

The courts keep to themselves, after all. The Seelie Hegemony still stands, but that doesn't mean the Blessed Courts don't hold a dagger to each other's throats even as they're promising smiles.

"It's still incredibly risky," I breathe, though my mind is whirring with thoughts and plans.

The Wraith King holds up one of the glittering soul-traps he wears around his neck. Inside it glows that silvery pale spark, an amorphous wisp of shape trapped inside its crystal prison.

Stolen from me the day I was cut from my fae mother's womb.

"Bring me back the Dragon's Heart," he purrs, leaning forward on his throne, "and I will grant you the rest of your soul."

Freedom.

He'll never be able to wield it against me, never hold it over my head again. I sense Soraya's head turn sharply to track me. She too is bound by such a trap. She too hungers.

Now I know why she wanted the job.

"Done." The word is on my lips before I can even think it through.

Soraya shoves to her feet. "A dangerous task to risk on someone so unworthy. Perhaps you think her the best for the challenge, but to send Zemira alone could be dangerous.

Let me go too—as her maid perhaps. They'll expect at least one attendant."

And she'll be there to steal the job the second she gets a chance.

"Your skills at dissembling are meager at best," I shoot back. "You'll give me away before I take two steps—"

"So we're to pin all our hopes on you?" she sneers.

"Tell me again: How *is* the Lord of Mistmark? Still alive? Still breathing? Why is that?"

Soraya takes a step toward me, fists clenched, but I face her just as determinedly. All the bloody years between us rise like vengeful ghosts. Sisters are both your greatest strength and greatest weakness. Only she can get close enough to deliver a merciless strike, because some part of me will always let her, every time. She's broken my heart a dozen times, and I, no doubt, the same.

But this time, I can see the blood drawn is hers.

And that makes me wonder, just a little, about the Lord of Mistmark.

Who should be dead.

Because my sister speaks the truth.

She is the best. She does not fail.

Raesh examines us both, a small smile crossing his mouth. "An excellent proposition, Soraya. You will attend your sister, though you will not hamper her." He tilts his head to me. "This is why you were born," the king replies. "Don't fail me."

I wouldn't dare.

Because Keir is not the only dangerous trap I have to avoid.

Now I have Soraya to contend with too.

2

"You said it wouldn't kill her," I hiss, as the sound of someone dying floats down the stairs of the inn in Hawkesbury Shrewd.

"Her ladyship's retching. Not dying," Soraya replies. "And her guards will bring the local herb woman to tend her. She'll recognize the smell of Monksflower and diagnose her with a nice peaceful two weeks in bed to recover. Perfect amount of time for us to get into the court, steal the Dragon's Heart, and get out."

"Oh, of course. An easy little trot," I reply snidely. "Nothing to worry about at all."

"Move," Soraya whispers harshly, shoving me in the back. "We haven't got all day."

Poisoning a Fae princess is probably the lowest I'm prepared to sink to avenge my family and protect my people.

Probably.

But then the Lady of Greenslieves has the one thing I need to pull off this entire caper.

An invitation.

The Dragon's Heart is one of the most powerful relics

ever crafted, the stories say. It anchors the Court of Dreams to the mortal plane, so that the court can come and go at will, the Wraith King told me. Strong enough to break the curse on my people and vicious enough to turn its wrath upon the Seelie Hegemony.

We'd no longer be trapped beyond the Shadowfangs. No longer cursed to a miserable half-life.

But if I succeed, this will mean war, and I'm not certain how I feel about that.

A bloody war ahead of me, all for the price of my soul. I shouldn't care. The fae hunt my kind. Long ago, I might have dreamed that they'd spare me for the half of my blood that belongs to them, but those dreams have long since turned to dust.

I'm not fae.

Not with even a whisper of my father's taint in my veins. I'm the monster that cost my mother her life, to be hunted and destroyed.

They'll never forget it.

"Stay here and guard the stairs," I mutter.

"Like a little servant bitch."

"You wanted to come."

Rolling my eyes, I step into the shadows beneath the stairs and *twist* through them until I'm slipping into the shadows inside the Lady Merisel's room.

This is the fun part.

The room opens up around me, draped in veils of darkness that steal all but the brightest light from the world. Nobody can see me here in the shadows, though I dare not step into the patch of sunlight that gilds the wooden floors.

Shadow Walking's an old, rare gift passed down through my father's bloodlines. Few wield it these days. Lucky me.

We weren't always wraiths.

Over three thousand years ago, the Dragon Wars obliterated most of my people. Those that survived were exiled from the Fair Lands and found shelter in the harsh, inhospitable mountains they call the Shadowfangs.

The Forbidden, they name us, though we once bore another.

The Unblessed.

The Courts of fae and beastkin alike, where no fae was too hideous, too twisted, too imperfect to be accepted. Unlike the shining, glittering Courts of the Blessed, where perfection is revered and the powerful rule with an iron fist.

Our imperfections cost us.

King Anselm of the Court of Dawn was the first to proclaim us tainted. He urged the Blessed Courts to wipe our "blight" from the world and formed the Seelie Hegemony against us.

The Unblessed fought to hold on to their lands, but Anselm fashioned a powerful weapon that drained the fae magic from our flesh and cost us the war.

One by one, the dark fae fell, until my grandfather, Prince Rakulh, used his darker magics to curse us into a new form. Not quite fae. Not quite dark fae. Faded from our past grandeur, our immortal lives forever lost to us, along with our most dangerous magic.

He was the first wraith.

And as the years passed and the curse crippled him, he died with a pledge on his lips: *One day the Forbidden will rise again and retake our lands.*

One day, the war will start again.

But to do that we need the strength to shatter King Anselm's weapon.

Shadow Walking is a fae gift. An Unseelie gift.

One that shouldn't exist in my mortal body following

the Purge, though my father finally found a means to circumvent the curse that restricts us.

And if any fae of the glittering courts knew I had the gift, they'd hunt me down and obliterate me.

The sour stink of vomit fills the air as I ripple through shadows, searching the room. Soraya and I have spent more than enough hours listening to Lady Merisel and her maids chattering about how excited they are about the Summons to know we're not looking for an actual invitation.

No, we need a charm.

Imbued with enough of Prince Keir's magic to protect its bearer from the lash of the portal's magic, it serves to keep the uninvited from attempting to penetrate his court.

For a second, I almost feel a moment of pity for poor Merisel. When this goes down, she'll be blamed.

Then I catch the glint of fine golden thread twined across her gowns, and the spill of silk and golden jewels that tumble from her travelling trunk.

Merisel is Blessed.

She's never known a moment of pain or torture in her life. Never had half her soul stolen from her. Never been hunted purely for the mistake of her birth or the ghostly luminescence of her skin.

I pluck the golden charm—the one that will protect me from the portal's magic—from beneath her jewelry box. The second I touch it, it evaporates into the shadows with me, and I tuck it inside my leather waistcoat.

Immortality and power beckon. Freedom.

And if that means war, then so be it.

The Blessed deserve it.

∾

THE COURT of Dreams is like nothing I expected.

The portal spits me out in the ancient glade of a forest. A waterfall plunges into a deep, dark hole bedecked in ferns and lush lilies, and I roll to a halt beside it in the leaf mulch. An ancient carving of the Goddess of Mercy looms out of the greenery, though her pale, marble skin is sheathed in a gown of moss, and her weathered face holds the wisdom of millennia.

Behind me the portal hums, its opaque surface rippling like sunlight over water. I haul myself to my feet, brushing off my borrowed finery.

And suddenly realize I'm not alone.

"It seems Prince Keir has invited practically *anybody*," says a haughty voice. "And here I thought this Summons was exclusive."

Fae ladies titter like a flock of starlings as the speaker glides toward me, bearing down upon me like a warship.

Half a dozen of them are gathered there in colorful gowns and crowns woven of gold and pearls, thorns and brambles. Several retainers await, wearing tufted ears that flicker, or tails that curl around their legs. It's a sign of their half-blood, and though they may strive to rise through the courts, they'll never climb higher than where they are.

The Blessed revere their pure blood.

And spit on those without it.

Clearly, today is the day to arrive and I'm to be the innocent lamb led to the slaughter.

"Don't worry," I mutter, "I'm sure the prince will be able to see exactly how well-*bred* you are."

The fae princess's eyes narrow on me. She's beautiful in an unearthly, inhuman kind of way. They always are. Tumbles of ruby-red hair are woven into an intricate crown, revealing the razor-sharp edge of her cheekbones and her glittering gold eyes. When she smiles, sharp teeth glint in the light.

All the better for tearing shreds off poor unsuspecting passers-by.

"Who are you?" she demands.

"Lady Merisel of Greenslieves." The lie rolls off my tongue as smoothly as honey. One of the gifts of the Forsaken's curse. We're no longer bound by the rules that govern the fae.

One could be mistaken for thinking the flock of princesses watching me harmless in their silks and braids, but their eyes hold the hungry look of a starving tiger. This is a Summons, which means none of us are friends. The challenge is to survive the court—and bring down the prize.

Who just happens to be a powerful, ancient fae male.

"And yourself?" I ask.

"You don't know who she is?" demands an incredulous blonde at her side.

"I don't know who any of you are," I reply.

The pair of them exchanges a look, and the redhead smiles nastily. "Greenslieves is a demesne far from its nearest court—and civilization. Lady Merisel's lack of knowledge is not surprising, Narcissa."

Princess Narcissa of the Court of Blood. Her uncle, King Aswan, rules the court, and it's said she's hungry to over-throw him.

Of all the Blessed fae, the Court of Blood ranks as one of the worst. It wouldn't surprise me if sweet Narcissa spends her time pulling the wings off demi-fae.

Not to be outdone, the redhead sneers at my plain green skirts. "I am Princess Ismena of the Storm Court."

Ah, just my luck.

Prince Angmar's vicious sister, Ismena, wearing a net of seaweed and pearls in her red hair.

If she recognizes me, I'm dead.

Ismena circles me, looking me up and down. There's no denying her gown is far finer than the one I stole from Lady Merisel, but I hold my chin high. "A worm from the forests," she says with a smirk. "The prince must have been desperate."

"You should return home," Narcissa adds. "You're outclassed and outbred here, worm."

I sense Soraya joining me, though she's more than adept at remaining in the shadows and avoiding notice.

Pity I cannot entirely say the same.

A raw impotent hate burns deep in my belly. The job is simple: get into the Court of Dreams, get the Dragon's Heart, and get out. A smart thief knows better than to draw attention. But I've spent twenty-eight years bowing my head to Blessed fae who think they're better than me. Every time, it chafes, but this time there's a rawness to the wound that will not be denied.

Fuck it. They all think I'm a fae lady, anyway. Why not show my claws?

"Outbred?" I mutter. "And here I thought it was inbred?"

Several of the other young princesses gasp. One smiles, though she pretends to hide it. I like her already.

Narcissa's face pales with fury. "You wretched little—"

A horn suddenly sounds, cutting off the words, though from the way she bites down on her lip, I know her sudden silence won't last.

Horses pour over the hill. A dozen guards in gleaming gold armor guard the party, and there are servants in the blue livery of the Court of Dreams. Saved by the arrival of the prince's greeting party, though there's no sign of the prince himself.

Every princess sweeps to their station, fixing errant curls of hair and adding crowns of flowers or gold. This is a competition, after all.

Soraya slinks past me, "I thought your plan was to draw no attention?"

"I changed my mind," I murmur as she hauls the trunk we "borrowed" from Merisel. "It seems the Lady of Greenslieves has an arrogant streak. And they're all here to win the prince's heart, no matter whom they have to trample. I think a glimpse of my claws might keep them off my back."

"If I were you, I'd be more worried about the knife they'll embed in it."

I shoot her a cool glance. "That's why I have you, sister dear. You don't think you're here just to sweep my chambers and empty the chamber pot?"

Soraya's teeth gleam, and suddenly I realize it's not just the princesses I'll have to keep an eye on. "Empty your own cursed chamber pot. You and I must work together, but don't forget that we're not allies."

I never do.

I learned that lesson in the training camps many, many years ago.

3

The Captain of the Guards watches me with the glittering attention of a hawk circling its prey from far above. In a sea of glimmering silks and tittering laughs, he knows I don't truly belong.

So do I.

Sweat drips down my spine as I hold the curtsy. Head bowed like a penitent, knees starting to shake, my hands sweeping the Lady of Greenslieves' fine silk skirts into a gush of fabric around me, I am the very picture of submission.

It's been years since I was trained for this.

I'm older than most of the other princesses, my manners stiff and ill-formed, like a thin veneer over the unpolished heart of me. Ismena hinted that she considers Greenslieves to be a backwater holding, so I'll use that to cover any gaffes, but I can't help thinking the captain looks at me longer than he does the others.

"Welcome to the Court of Dreams," calls the seneschal who accompanied us to the palace. "Tonight there shall be a welcoming dinner. In the meantime, please avail yourselves of the wine and candied sweetmeats, though you're quite welcome to use the time to refresh yourselves in your rooms."

Servants flood the courtyard, offering trays and goblets that are filled to the brim. The sweet scent of magnolias fills the air, and fountains splash and burble. As far as courts go, it's impressive. I can see the palace's domes over the golden sandstone walls that lock us in here, but so far the Court of Dreams has earned its title.

"Any sign of him yet?" I mutter to Soraya.

"Someone's watching us," she murmurs.

"No doubt surveying the flock of prizes that await him."

It's time to see if this ruse will pay off.

They say the Prince of Dreams can see through magic itself and pierce any lie with the cold, locking stare he's said to have perfected. Let's see if he can see through my glamour.

The herald raps his staff on the hard tiles and begins to call out Prince Keir's titles. Lord of the Morning Star, Prince of Chaos and Dreams, Master of Nightmares.... It's a mouthful, and I cannot resist rolling my eyes as the herald drones on. Who needs so many names?

I only have one: Zemira Az Ghul.

But once there were others, gifted to me by my mother upon my birth, before they were stolen by my father, along with the rest of me.

Zemira Ashburn. Gravekissed, the Black Hawk, Winterborn.

The fae do so love their titles. They collect them like rare antiques, and I can't help wondering if it's a means to hide other, ahem, shortcomings.

Bare feet whisper over the marble floors.

None of the other princesses notice, but I can feel the

prickle of hot eyes watching me. Maybe it's just the thought of being caught out, but every nerve I own is on edge.

A thief knows when she's being watched.

I turn, and there's the Prince of Dreams himself, stalking toward me with sinuous grace.

Dark hair flows to his shoulders, but it's those thick, dark brows that give his green-gold eyes an intensity that almost makes me back away a step. He moves with the loose-hipped stride of a predator, and I can practically feel the coil of alien power simmering beneath his olive skin.

Skin that's very much on show.

His chest is bare, a long, loose robe of midnight flowing from his shoulders and a golden claw hanging about his throat. Trousers sit low on his hips, revealing the chiseled cut of muscle that dips into dangerous terrain. Every inch of him is expertly forged, and any female would want to explore.

Even me.

Sweet Mother of Mercy. I'd been prepared for a fae prince, but what I hadn't expected was the sheer primordial power practically spilling from his pores.

I am so fucked.

It's as if he senses my sudden nerves.

His head turns, hunting through the crowd of princesses as if he's caught the edge of my errant thought. This must be how it feels to be stalked by a wolf. The other females are merely collateral damage. He's searching for the right prey. The weakest link. The straggler.

And the second he spots me, I know it's me.

The Prince of Dreams's eyes devour every inch of me, as if I'm nothing more than a tasty morsel to consume. "The Lady of Greenslieves, I presume?"

My breath catches in my chest, as if someone's punched me there.

"None other." I have no idea how I force my voice to work. His presence weaves its own magic.

"Tell me? Does your father still hold to the Old Traditions?"

I have no idea. "He does his best, my prince."

Keir searches my eyes, though I'm not sure what he's looking for. I can sense the others watching, little whispers catching the edge of my consciousness, but for a second, I cannot look away.

"Then you are welcome here." It's a soft murmur, and I cannot stop the shivers that tremble down my arms.

The second he looks away from me, I release a breath. That was... intense. For a second, the thought of what I intend overwhelms me.

Steal from this prince? Am I insane?

Desperate, I tell myself.

Fine. He's powerful. All the fae are.

I have to remind myself of what's at stake.

I picture that little crystalline soul-trap around my father's throat.

The Wraith King didn't breed Soraya or me out of the kindness of his heart. He has none. No, he's the kind of creature that plays a long game, and for nearly fifty years he's been focused on breeding a half-fae, half-wraith child that can pass among the courts.

Of all those bastards found in the training camps, there were but a handful that displayed more fae qualities than wraithenkind. It didn't grant us any advantage. Indeed, the others knew we were the chosen ones, and they outnumbered us three to one. I'd often wake to a hand over my mouth and a blade to my throat and swiftly learned to sleep lightly.

And to keep a knife under my pillow.

I don't know who my mother was.

Some highborn fae from one of the northern courts, I think. Raesh used to send raiding parties out to capture the purebloods for his breeding purposes. When my birth went poorly, he ordered me cut from my mother's womb, and I don't know her fate.

Only the whisper of my true name in my ears; a name meant for me and me alone.

Sometimes I hear it in my dreams, and I wonder what she was like. Was she frightened of what she'd been sentenced to? Did she despise me for the act of my begetting? Or did she love me and hope to free me one day?

I'll never know.

My loyalty is bound to my father by magic—not love or familial affection. And I would do anything to escape its trap.

Even this.

My resolves firms as I watch the Prince of Dreams greet each princess in kind. He's dangerous and powerful, but he's the key to my freedom.

All I have to do is find his relic and steal it.

And maybe then I'll have a chance to discover more about my mother's people and who she was.

"WELL," says a voice by my side. "He's everything I've ever heard said of him. Whoever captures his attention is bound to find a wild ride. That prince won't take to the bit well."

It's the female who smiled when I called Narcissa

inbred. Her hair is a riot of golds and reds, with a crown of brambles woven through it, but it's her eyes that are her most defining feature. They're the gold of a hawk's eyes, and her brows fan over them with a hint of a feathery curl.

She looks nothing like the others, in their silks and precious gems. Instead, she's wearing a gown of reddened autumn leaves threaded with thin gold chains.

"Whoever thinks *they're* going to land *him* has another think coming." We both watch the prince, and I shake my head. "He's playing his own games here."

"Aren't we all?" She snorts.

And I glance at her a little more closely.

"Calliope of the Forest of Thistlewood," she says, in response to my unspoken question.

One of the Wild Fae who are owned by no court.

If anyone belongs here as uneasily as I do, it's her.

"The worm," I reply dryly, for that's what Narcissa and her friends have named me. "Though my friends may call me Merisel of Greenslieves."

"I think I'll call you Merisel," she says, scanning the gaggle of princesses who surround the prince, "as you have more than your share of enemies."

"You've noticed."

Another faint smile. "Pay them no mind. Narcissa's fighting for an ally to help her win her throne from her uncle, and Ismena needs to protect her brother's court. Apparently, Angmar's powers wane with the loss of his trident, and he has wolves poised at every door."

"Desperate means dangerous."

This time, there's a hint of a predator in her eyes. "I'm well guarded against their claws. And they've spent too much time in a *civilized* court. They forget what it means to be the darkness in the forest. The huntress who bares her teeth. They're merely pretty dolls playing at court games, and when it comes time for bloodletting, they'll find my bite is worse than my bark."

Don't cross the Wild Fae is an old, well-known saying.

She looks at me. "But you're not a pretty doll. I can see the hunger in your eyes, and the baring of your teeth in every smile. We should be friends, you and I."

"Until the end?" I murmur, well aware that Calliope is playing her own games.

"An alliance until we're the last two standing?"

It won't hurt to have someone watching my back.

Until she thinks it time to remove me from the field of play.

"To hunting princes," I reply, with a smile.

"To hunting princes."

4

The first chance I get, I steal away through the palace to scope the lay of the land.

It's oddly silent in the lamp-lit hallways, and as I slip through them, I silently place myself on the mental map I have of the palace. Throne room, audience chamber, the gallery, the promenade.... There has to be a way to the lower floors where the treasury is sure to be. If anyone asks, I'll claim I'm lost.

Laughter echoes from above, startling me.

Apparently the prince is entertaining tonight.

Auditioning, I should say.

He's made it clear he expects to end this entire ruse with a pretty princess by his side, and the entire flock of them is awash with predatory intent. They look like a herd of flamingoes in their finery, albeit flamingoes with sharp teeth and hidden claws. Four of them have already formed some sort of alliance—Narcissa and Ismena among them—and they've made two girls cry. If I had to listen to their whispered malice for the evening, I was going to do something rash.

Like stick a knife in someone.

If I were Prince Keir, I would lock my bedroom doors. One or two of those princesses look desperate to me. And desperate is dangerous.

Stairs beckon ahead of me, leading down into the gloom. *Yes*. Here we are. Glancing along the hallway, I find myself alone. Slipping from shadow to shadow—old habits die hard—I'm almost standing at the top of them when something moves behind me; a whisper of noise, like that of silk rasping over stone.

Spinning around, I stare along the hallway.

Lights flicker in their sconces. Two of them further down the hall have been extinguished, but there's no one there.

A hint of dread trickles inexplicably down my spine, but maybe it's naught more than the thrill of getting caught?

And then a shadow moves, huge and towering. It ripples along the hallway and it moves fast.

Damn it.

Hauling up a fistful of my skirts, I turn and bolt around one of the enormous columns that line the hallways, slamming directly into a firm, hard chest—

Hands immediately lock around my upper arms, and my weight shifts onto the balls of my feet, instinct preparing me to throw him.

And that's when I see his face, hard and implacable.

The perfect straight line of his nose. The cut of those hawkish cheekbones.

The prince himself.

"What are you doing here?" I gasp, because tossing the Lord of the Morning Star, the Master of Chaos, and Lord of Shadows—or was it Secrets?—onto his backside is probably not the best idea.

One of those dark eyebrows lift. "I should say the same. This is my palace. I'll skulk behind columns if I wish to."

I can't help myself. A smile curves my lips. "Hiding from your flock of pursuers?"

"The question is: What are you doing here?"

I bat my lashes at him. "Hoping to ensnare a certain handsome fae in my web"—his smile widens—"only to have you stumble into it instead."

I make a sound of disgust, and the prince actually laughs.

He lets me go, one thumb stroking the tender inner skin of my elbow, but as his laughter fades, those dark eyes dart over me and I realize he's not fooled. I didn't answer his question, and he knows it.

"I was trying to find the rose gardens," I admit. "They say the palace is beautiful, but the gardens are... another thing entirely. After dinner, I felt the need for some fresh air."

Away from the syrupy sweet threats thrown my way and the pathetic way some of the princesses have been trying to capture Prince Keir's attention. Calliope chose to stay. I think some part of her enjoys watching them pander to him.

"Then you are going the wrong way," he says.

"Was I?" Oh, the horror.

Prince Keir seems to make some sort of decision. With a dangerous smile, he holds out his hand. "Let me escort you."

This is... not ideal.

"Don't you have princesses to pursue?"

"Perhaps I'm pursuing one right now?"

For some strange reason, it seems I've caught his attention. *Of course.* I almost close my eyes and slap my own forehead. I'm the one female not at the gathering tonight. The one female *not* trying to crawl into his lap.

And he's the typical predatory fae male.

They prefer to be the pursuer, not the pursued.

I just posted an enormous glowing dare above my head.

Perhaps I can scare him off?

"I would just *love* to explore the gardens with you," I say in a voice dripping with sweetness as I accept his arm. "What lady would not care for such delightful, *exclusive* company?"

It's clear he doesn't quite know what to make of this statement as he leads me toward the gardens. I burble a handful of answers to his vague questions on the way, careful to smile a little too widely and bat my eyelashes whenever he looks at me.

I'll make him regret this little sojourn.

Fey lanterns glimmer through the trees. Leashed lightning, they call it, and it casts a soft blue glow over everything.

Once again, the shock of his appearance takes my breath.

He towers over me by a good five inches.

His eyes seem laced with silver tonight, instead of their usual gold. Lightning dances in those stormy depths, hinting at the turbulence within, as he watches me. "What do you think? Do the gardens hold up to your expectations?"

We're not talking about gardens.

"The gardens are *everything* I expected them to be."

"You seem disappointed."

"I'm not. The Court of Dreams is lovely." I turn to a rose and brush my fingers over its satiny petals. "It's just.... It doesn't feel real, in some way. Everything's too perfect. There are no blemishes. No slight imperfections. Did you notice every rose has the exact same number of petals? And not a single thorn. This is a dreamscape, isn't it? You created this."

As if to prove my point, the golden medallion around his throat winks in the light. "Yes. You do not like it?"

"Of course I like it. It's perfection. But it's not real."

"You're not interested in illusions?" he asks as he steps closer.

"I'm not interested in lies."

Reaching out, he brushes his hands over my eyes, and I close them. Thumbs caress my eyelids, but it's not merely a sensuous feeling. It feels like he's brushing cobwebs from my eyes.

"Open," he whispers, "and see the truth."

Color drains from the world around us as I blink. The fine details smudge, the lines blur, and then.... Then I'm looking at a world of imperfection. The roses still nod and beckon, but they're no longer uniformly perfect. Crushed petals roam underfoot. Vines snake up the cracked stone walls that enclose the garden.

It's wild and untamed, and still beautiful.

Perhaps even more so, for its realness.

"Oh, my," I reply, taking two unsteady steps forward and trailing my fingers over the petals. "How much of this place was created by you?"

"All of it," he replies, and there's something in his eyes as he looks across the gardens himself. "Haven't you realized why it's so difficult to get into the Court of Dreams? It's not real. It's a world within a world, and I rule it."

"Just as difficult to escape it, I presume?"

His smile holds an edge. "If I will it, yes. It is not merely dreams I can twist."

Nightmares, too.

Wraith's balls. I just walked into a trap. One that can snap closed at any moment.

Wrapping my arms around myself, I stride to the edge of

the balcony that juts out from the mountainside. Lush shadowy lands stretch out below. Glittering lights from the town far below. "Am I even really here, or am I asleep in that glade? Is this all in my head?"

Are you in my head?

"Pinch yourself," he suggests.

It's ridiculous, but I do. A flare of pain skitters through my nerves. *Real.* Some of the tension leeches out of me. If it's real, then I can escape it.

"I've been here over three thousand years, Merisel. The world has grown more real over time, imprinted with my every thought, my every desire." Which would explain the nubile serving girls. "Even without me, it would still exist. The Court of Dreams has taken on substance over the years. Weight. These lands are real now, though woven of magic, with pure Chaos as its bedrock. It's an Other World."

Other Worlds are the stuff of legends.

Spun into reality by the dreams of dragons, they're dangerous, alluring places. The dragons are all gone now, slumbering forever in the stone of the earth. But the worlds remain.

You can reach them only by portal, and you must obey the laws that rule them. Dangerous lands. Dangerous courts. Entering one could cost you your life—or gift you with riches so powerful, you will forever live a blessed life.

And this one no less so, ruled by a prince so powerful he's managed to create it himself.

A shiver runs down my spine. The Dragon's Heart must be even more powerful than I imagined. No mere fae could create something like this.

"Are you trying to avoid me?" he murmurs suddenly. "I noticed you went out of your way to sit at the other end of the table at dinner."

It's the first time I've looked at him since he removed the glamour from my eyes.

Not a damned thing has changed about his face.

Ugh. It was not an illusion.

Why couldn't he have had something lopsided about his smile, or his eyes less luster? "I'm not avoiding you."

His smile stretches as if he senses my displeasure. "Then you have some issue with this face? You rarely look at me."

"No issue. You're definitely the prettiest in all the lands," I say, referencing the old story about a long-shattered court and a magic mirror.

He laughs. But it swiftly fades. "Prettiest?"

Oh, so someone doesn't like that?

"You would make an exceptionally handsome match with the Lady Altrea. Or perhaps the Princess Ismena. Anyone beholding the pair of you would be blinded by your beauty."

If not by Ismena's venom.

"You do not count yourself among such ranks?"

"A lowly lady like myself does not dare dream."

He steps forward as if to pursue me. "But that is the purpose of a Summons. Every female here tonight has a chance."

I glance across the gardens, wrapping my arms around myself. I'd hoped not to capture his attention, for twisting my way through wordplay is not my best asset. *Be bland.* "You're too kind."

"But you don't want a chance," he swiftly notes.

Damn it. It's a fine line I walk. *Don't capture his attention, but don't have him dismiss you either.* "Of course, I do. It would be a coup for my family. A strong alliance with a powerful court."

All things he'd expect me to say.

"*Lie*," he whispers, as if he can taste it on my tongue.

"It's not a lie," I protest.

The prince reaches out and touches the tip of his finger just beneath my chin, forcing me to meet his eyes. They blaze, full of mercurial temper. "Now you're insulting me."

"I mean no insult."

A dangerous smile touches his mouth. "That one tastes a little like the truth, though it's not entirely there. Yet. It makes me curious. You have no liking for this Summons. Do you know what I think?" he murmurs.

"What?"

"I think, for all your talk of illusion and lies, you shroud yourself in them."

It strips the smile from my lips. "*What?*"

"You play courtier with a honeyed tongue. You dodge and deflect with assured grace. Every word you've spoken tonight has been a misdirect, a gilded statement." He leans closer, and my back meets the wall. There's nowhere to go. "You're not the only one who's not interested in lies, my lady. Why are you here if not for me? What does the Lady Merisel want?"

Probably to stop retching.

He's good. And I cannot afford for him to rescind the invitation. Not just yet. I've barely had a chance to look around. If he can pluck the lie from my tongue, then I need to get better at deflecting him. "Perhaps she wants freedom?"

He stares at me for a long, slow minute.

And then he nods.

"It's not that I'm not flattered, my prince," I swiftly say. "But... I'm not entirely certain an alliance between us serves my interests. You seek a bride, and no doubt when you find her, you intend for her to live here with you. You're a powerful prince who rules this entire court, but what would your bride become?"

"She would sit at my right hand."

"And would she be free to make her own choices? Her own decisions? Would she rule jointly, or would she be your plaything?"

His brow furrows. "I have no interest in pretty playthings."

"But you haven't thought about it," I press, tipping my chin up higher. "You have us all dancing to your tune, but what would change when one of us becomes victor? Would I be free to come and go as I please? What does the Prince of Dreams want? What role does *he* see his bride fulfilling?"

"What do I want? A queen to serve at my side, to rule forever with me. And she would have her freedom, to a degree, as long as she knew she was *mine*."

"But would you be hers?" I whisper.

His gaze drops to my lips. Hands press against the wall on either side of my waist.

Nowhere to go. No escape.

Only the hard cage of his body.

"I would be hers," he promises. "Forever and always. If she gave me her trust, she would have mine. If she gave me her heart, she would have mine. If she gave me her soul...."

Her soul.

Panic flares within me. Of all the things he could ask for, he cannot have that. I don't even own it myself. Yet.

"But would you be the first to offer your heart?" I whisper. "Or would you demand hers first? You speak of trust, but I'm not entirely certain you can give it."

"Three thousand years is a long time to know the kiss of betrayal."

And that's all I can offer him.

I close my eyes, breathing in the nearness of his body. "A heart—a soul—is no mere thing to trifle with. Without trust, can either be given?"

The shadows pull at me, and I'm surprised by how strong the urge to flee is. It's just a man. Just a prince. Just a promise of carnality.

He wouldn't be the first I've twisted around my finger, though it's the first time I've wanted to play back. And that bothers me a little.

"Can I trust your intentions," he muses, "when you seed your truths with lies? Can I trust your keenness when you admit you have doubts? When your father no doubt pushed you to accept this invitation?"

"Can I trust my prince when he offers me the world but admits there are conditions? As for truth, you asked me why I'm here." Heart pounding at his nearness, I glance up. "I'm here to see if I can steal your heart. It's the only thing I'm interested in."

His eyes narrow. "That almost sounds like truth."

That's because it is.

I just didn't say which heart I meant.

Pressing a hand to his bare chest, I almost gasp at the heat of his skin. His pulse races beneath my palm.

What would it be like to allow this?

To let him steal a kiss?

It isn't in the plan.

But for just one moment, I long for it.

What would it be like to know love? To know trust? They're words woven of golden dreams, but they tempt like nothing else can.

Even as they ruin me.

There can be nothing but betrayal between us. One day

this male will be my enemy. I despise the role my father has forced upon me, because what the prince wants is tempting.

I have known nothing but betrayal my entire life.

I have become its instrument, and I hate what the Wraith King has wrought of me. What is the price of a soul? The downfall of another? War? Death?

Hate?

I can bear these things, for the taste of freedom is even more tempting than the idea of this dark prince's heart. But the thought burns, set ablaze in my chest.

Prince Keir must see the hint of longing in my eyes, for he leans down and his lips come into focus for the first time all night. For such a harsh, intense face, his mouth is pure softness, pure sin. I freeze as I realize exactly what he intends.

But it's not with horror.

All of that heat cages me in, my breasts suddenly straining for the press of his chest to mine. It's been years since I've tasted the flesh of another's body or danced that wicked dance.

His breath whispers over my sensitive lips, and I realize I'm going to allow this. Worse. I intend to relish every moment of it—

And that's when the screaming starts.

5

Welcome e jerk apart, and suddenly blood rushes back into my brain. What was I even thinking? Or was I thinking at all? For none of this was in the plan.

Saved by someone's scream.

"Stay there!" Keir snarls, and then he's vanishing into the gardens, sprinting toward the castle.

Fae males and their arrogance. Oh, let me swoon.

I haul my skirts up and find one of the blades strapped to my thigh. More screams are pealing through the air. Perhaps Soraya grew weary of waiting for me. Maybe she's slaughtering that precious flock of doves inside.

Or maybe Ismena or Narcissa had the poor sense to mock my sister.

One can hope.

But even as I sprint toward the palace, I know I'm not going to be that lucky.

Blood splashes the marble floors of the hallway, and there's a long, bloody mark where someone tried to crawl away. The clash of swords echoes ahead of me, and there's this horrible, awful snarling sound that sends a chill down my spine.

I don't know where Keir's gone, but he's most likely headed directly to where the sounds of fighting echo.

Stalking along the hallway, I hold myself right on the edge of the Sift, just in case I need to get away suddenly.

One step around the next corner and I'm confronted with a sight directly from my nightmares. Lady Altrea stares blankly at the ceiling, her throat torn out and the skin around it bleached of all color. She was one of the females in Narcissa and Ismena's alliance, and though I wasn't fond of her, no one deserves this.

I kneel beside her, closing those cerulean eyes even as I examine the wound. There's something not right about it. Long, bloodied gouges like teeth marks have torn her throat right out. But it's the grayed edges that look unnatural, as if something's tainted the flesh.

A grunt huffs through the hallway behind me, and every hair along my spine rises.

I'm not alone.

Spinning to my feet, I catch a glimpse of a creature warped of pure shadows stalking toward me. It lifts its muzzle to the moon and howls.

A Wyrdwolf. Twice the size of me and covered in dense black tufts of fur. A ruddy light glows behind the cage of its bleached ribs, as if its heart is forged with the light of a dying star. It looks like it has crawled out of some grave somewhere, and its putrid breath fogs the air, stinking of rot.

A nightmare twisted directly from the Shadow Realms. After all, the Court of Dreams is but one Other World. There are more. And they're not all as pretty as this one.

"Mother of Night, protect me," I whisper, taking a stealthy step back as the Wyrdwolf advances.

No Sifting will save me now. Wyrdwolves have the ability to Shadow Walk too.

It ripples toward me, red eyes glowing and its bloodied maw dripping crimson with Altrea's blood.

I hold the knife low. Good, cold iron crafted by a goblin smith that fused pure shadows to the blade. It can cut through anything, but as I see more of the Wyrdwolf, I'm suddenly not so certain of that. Iron can kill any of the fae. I have to hope it will be enough.

Shouts echo behind it.

The Wyrdwolf's ears flicker back, and then it launches forward, aiming for my throat.

I Sift to the side, my iron raking along those rotten ribs. And then I throw myself forward into a roll, momentarily thanking every master in the training camps for pushing my body to the brink all those years ago.

There's no time to think or dwell. Only time to move. Every animal instinct I own is telling me to get out of there, but what if it follows me through the shadows?

"Merisel!" someone yells, and then the prince is there, striding along the hallway with his robe flaring wide behind him.

His skin is gilded with light as his magic spills out of him, and it glows in his eyes. Keir twists his hands, and golden chains shoot out from his palms, lashing around the Wyrdwolf's legs.

I roll under its abdomen, slashing up with the knife and spilling hot entrails across the floor. Then I'm gagging as the stink of it hits my nostrils with the force of a runaway carriage. *I didn't get any of it on me, did I?*

"Get out of the way!" Keir snarls, weaving his hands together in a sinuous dance. The chains work their way around the creature's body, twisting brutally into shadow-born flesh.

Gladly.

I bolt to the side, but a vicious snap of teeth catches the hem of my skirt, and I go sprawling. No time to look. I have to move. Scrambling to my hands and knees, I slash through the ends of my skirt, and suddenly I'm free.

I can practically feel its hot breath on the back of my neck. I know I said I wouldn't Sift in front of Keir, but right now—

Just a blink. A slip in shadows.

A clash of fierce teeth over open air, right behind me.

I gain enough space to scramble free, though the fucking skirts are doing their best to betray me. How, by the light of the Cauldron, do fae princesses *do* anything in these blasted things?

The Wyrdwolf screams in animalistic rage as those chains bite deeper into its putrid flesh. Bones pop. Fur sizzles with the wet reek of something from the swamp. It bites and snaps at the chains cutting their way through its flesh, but then its red eyes lock on me as if it knows its not going to escape. As if it knows death is but a mere twist of Keir's hands away and it wants to take every last living thing with it.

I see my death in its eyes.

I scream, kicking backward across the floor as the Wyrd-wolf lunges for me, but then Keir is there. Hot golden light spills through the hallway, a flaming sword flickering to life in the prince's hands. It cleaves right through the Wyrd-wolf's neck, and the afterimage burns my retinas.

Blood spatters across my skirts as the head rolls across the floor. The Wyrdwolf's body slumps into a boneless mess on the floor, and as I watch, its blood seems to run together into puddles and its ribs cave in. The fire in its chest dies. Wherever it came from, without that fire, it's no longer bound to this plane.

Prince Keir kneels at my side, the sword evaporating into nothing. "Are you all right?" he demands.

"Fine." I stare at the dissolving puddle of sludge on the floor as I push to my feet. "What happened? How did that—?"

"I'll take care of it." He steps between me and what remains of the Wyrdwolf, as if he's hiding something. "Are you sure you're fine?"

Curse it. I forgot to swoon. No help for it now. "Well, as much as I enjoyed dinner, it *is* threatening to return with a vengeance. Apart from that—and the stink—I think I'll survive." I pause. "Thank you for the memorable evening."

The Prince of Dreams stares at me for a long, slow moment, and I have no idea what's going on behind those dangerous eyes. "Not quite what I had planned."

A smile escapes me. "You did get to show off your excellent skills with a blade and rescue the damsel from the nightmare. If I didn't smell like something that just died, I might be inclined to grant you a kiss."

"If a nightmare didn't just crawl out of the Shadow Realms and attack two of my guests, I might be inclined to accept it," he says in a dry voice.

Only a puddle of sludge remains on the floor. "How did it get here?"

There's that hesitation again, as if he knows more than he wants to reveal. "I'm sure my guards will perform a full investigation. You should clean yourself up and go to bed, Lady Merisel. I'll take care of this."

If I didn't smell like I'd rolled in a rotten carcass, I might take exception at being dismissed so readily. "As you wish, my prince."

An almost-kiss from Keir? Or the snap of a Wyrdwolf's jaws?

I don't know which one has proven more dangerous tonight.

∼

I RIPPLE through the shadows as Keir directs his servants to remove the mess in the hallway and see to the body.

Armored guards pour through the halls and the gardens, but I can't get close enough to hear what they're looking for. It's clear that nobody expected the Wyrdwolf to leap out of nowhere, and Keir's expression imitates a brewing storm. This is his court. His reputation on the line. Somehow he has to tell Lady Altrea's father that his daughter won't be coming home.

"How did it get in?" murmurs the Captain of the Guards, looking worried. "The safeguards are—"

"Impenetrable," Keir replies, kneeling by the body. He drapes his robe over Lady Altrea, hiding her from view and perhaps granting her a certain dignity. "I've checked. Nothing came through the portal."

"Then someone here opened a portal," says the captain.

"Or," Keir adds grimly, "we're dealing with someone who can twist the dream realm into flesh. This wasn't real. A true Wyrdwolf wouldn't have died so easily. It was dream-forged."

The captain falls silent.

Either way, it's not a pleasant thought.

To manipulate an Other World requires either a

dangerous sort of power—or a relic. It's also a direct challenge to the prince.

Perhaps I'm not the only one who took advantage of the Summons to attend. Every princess in the palace has their own agenda, after all, though I thought they were mostly benign.

But why would someone murder Lady Altrea?

Was she competition? Was it a grudge?

Why reveal their hand so swiftly? They have to know Prince Keir won't take kindly to the threat.

Unless.... Whoever did this has the power to twist a world Prince Keir controls. Maybe this is a deliberate taunt, and they intend to challenge the prince for his court.

Excellent. Sounds like I've walked directly into a war. It ought to be the perfect cover for my own intended crimes, but I can't help thinking the stakes suddenly got higher.

I Sift away through the shadows, seeking refuge in my own chambers.

Infiltrate the Court of Dreams, Father said. Steal the Dragon's Heart. It will be easy.

I shudder as I melt back into mortal flesh.

This task just became a thousand times more dangerous.

6

The next day, one could be forgiven for thinking anybody died within these walls.

Everybody is summoned to the audience chamber. It's far too early to be out of bed, let alone coherent, but I do my best, because the Lady Merisel would be just as thrilled as all the other females by the promise of time spent in the prince's company, even if she had to jostle for a place at his side. I might not have fooled Keir, but I cannot allow any of the princesses to start wondering why I'm here, if not for him.

I let them all crowd the prince.

No point fighting my way through that gauntlet of elbows and slippers stomping on my feet, just to catch a glimpse of his wit.

"I hear you managed to steal a moment alone with his Royal Studliness last night." Calliope appears at my elbow, and I didn't hear her coming. "Someone saw the two of you conversing in the hallway, and the Twisted Twins are up in arms. You ought to watch your back today."

"The Twisted Twins?"

"The leaders of the prince-hunting pack."

Ah. Ismena and Narcissa. I can't summon the hate today, however, for there's a gaping hole in their little coterie. Not that any of them look disconcerted by Altrea's death.

What if one of them summoned the creature? It would certainly explain the lack of concern.

"Did they happen to mention I was covered in Wyrdwolf gunk at the time?" I drawl wryly. "It took me three baths to get the wretched stink off me. Trust me. There was nothing romantic about it."

"Inconsequential details," she says, waving it away. "So what happened?"

I swiftly explain the night's events, leaving out the more interesting parts.

"A Wyrdwolf?" she asks dubiously. "Someone brought a Wyrdwolf into the court?"

"I believe the prince is investigating, and he's certainly roused his guards." There's an armor-plated guardian at every corner. "But you ought to watch your back, just in case." A thought occurs. "I'm not one for the courts. Do you know of anyone who might have borne Altrea a grudge?"

"You think it was summoned directly to kill her?"

"I don't know. Could be coincidence."

Calliope turns her gaze upon the other princesses. "Princess Altrea was of the Court of Fauna. I heard Narcissa call her a beast yesterday. There was no love lost between their courts—some old grudge, I think—but I don't know the specifics."

The princess of the Blood Court just keeps coming to my attention. Narcissa is cruel, but is she a killer? "Is she powerful enough to twist an Other World to her whim though?"

The sounds of excited gasps forestall Calliope's answer.

It takes a moment to work out what has them all so excited. Prince Keir has called for a hunt. Apparently we're all to go together; a chance for the prince to get to know us a little better.

Now the request to wear riding leathers makes sense.

Not that half the crowd has taken notice of it. There's more silk and ruffles around me than a milliner could boast.

"A hunt." Calliope screws her nose up. "I think I may abstain. There's been enough blood spilled of late." She heads toward the palace. "You'd be wise if you take my advice. I don't think any of us should be alone out there with... certain princesses."

I'm supposed to distract the prince today. Soraya wants a closer look at the palace. Besides, with so many guards suddenly at attention, the bright light of day is no place to make a move. Patience is a thief's best weapon, and there'll be plenty of time to make a move when the furor dies down. "I think I'll take my chances."

If Narcissa had anything to do with Altrea's death, then I want to know more.

We're led to the courtyard, where saddled horses await. Over a dozen vicious princesses fight for the most pleasing mount. I watch with faint amusement. Fae politics can be brutal, and I can't be bothered playing back.

I'm left with a fractious gray gelding named Ghost that tries to bite me when I take his reins. I snap my teeth at him. "Don't annoy me. It's barely a civilized hour."

"Not fond of morning?" Prince Keir murmurs as he leads his stallion past.

Of course it's enormous. And black, with a long silky mane and feathered fetlocks. One would think he had something to prove.

"I had trouble sleeping," I mutter. "I'm surprised you look

so cheerful this morning. Someone did summon a Wyrd-wolf to your castle, after all."

His smile doesn't slip. "And I will find them."

There's no time to ask more, because he's instantly surrounded by a swirl of lilac-scented silk.

"What are we hunting?" Princess Ismena calls as she whirls her bloodred bay in tight circles. She's one of the few in leather breeches and a trim little leather corset that displays her narrow waist to best effect.

"And what is the prize if we're the first to bring it down?" cries another princess, one with flowing blue hair that looks like she's just stepped out of the waves.

Keir swings into the saddle, his leather breeches creaking over his thighs. It's a sight to behold, despite the fact I should not be even looking in that direction. "The woods to the north are wild and untamed. They're the haunt of one of the last unicorns in the land. It's an ancient, mighty beast, and it can only be brought down by wiles."

Or a noose made from the hair of a virgin.

"Capture the unicorn," he calls, "and you will win a private dinner with me tonight."

The squeals are deafening.

The loosely knotted bridle hanging at my saddle suddenly makes sense. Some brunette somewhere has lost a length of hair.

"If I capture it, can I have its horn?" asks the Princess of the Dawn court.

Keir's smile fades, and I can sense that Princess Dawn just fell highly out of favor. "Am I not prize enough? It would be a shame to destroy such a mighty creature for the mere sake of a horn. No. If brought down, he'll be released at the end of the day. He is one of the last, after all."

It makes me like him a little more.

No beast should be hunted for the sake of a body part that cannot be eaten or used for warmth. Some say to grind a unicorn's horn into their drink will increase their fertility, but it's never been proven. And unicorns are rare creatures. There used to be more of them, but now all that's left is worthless scepters scattered through the fae courts.

"You should stay behind, worm," Princess Ismena hisses as she drives her bay into the path of my gelding. "You'll never capture his attention. You're not worthy of him."

It's a good thing I wasn't planning on winning.

But despite that fact, I cannot help snapping back, "I think it falls to the prince's whim to decide who's worthy."

She bears her teeth at me. "Don't get in my way."

"Or what?" I refuse to let her cow me. "Usually these warnings come with a threat."

Princess Ismena's smile is merciless. "Oh, I'd hate to ruin the surprise. Why don't you try me?"

Maybe I should convince Soraya that Ismena needs a good dose of bitterroot.

It might improve her personality.

CAPTURE THE UNICORN and win the company of the prince.

It's a prize I don't want. No. Hopefully one of the other princesses gains victory—and the precious dinner. With Keir distracted there's a chance to search his rooms.

But I hate the thought of Princess Ismena winning.

So, while I stay at the back of the pack as they gallop madly for the trees, I don't let Ghost fall too far behind.

Hours pass.

The darkhounds race ahead of us, slipping like shadows themselves through the trees as they hunt for any sign of the unicorn. The woods are old and tangled with thorns. Gnarled roots sprawl across the path, forcing me to keep my eye on what I'm doing. One princess has already fallen and been escorted back to the palace, though it's her horse I feel sorry for.

Ismena cuts me off on a narrow path, forcing me to rein the gray in hard. I don't want him to twist his leg, though she has no such compunctions.

"Give in, worm," she calls, using brute force to push me back.

I rein the gray in tight circles, and suddenly we're knee-to-knee. I grab her reins, just as a flash of light highlights the knife in her hand.

For a second I think she's going for my leg, but then I feel the saddle pitch sideways, threatening to take me with it. The bitch has cut my girth.

Ismena laughs as she kicks me in the chest. I try to grab Ghost's mane, but all I get is a handful of ethereal *nothing*. The virgin-hair bridle, damn it. I'm unceremoniously dumped on the ground. Thankfully, not into the vicious patch of brambles to my right.

A baying goes up. Clearly, they're on the scent of something.

Ghost bolts at the noise.

"Long walk home, worm," Ismena calls as she turns her horse in the direction of the cry. "I'll give your regards to the prince when I'm dining with him tonight."

Then she's gone, and I'm all alone in the middle of a shadowy forest with nothing but a fistful of virgin's hair.

"Cauldron's piss," I swear, kicking at the brambles.

There's no sign of Ghost, who's been aptly named. The bastard's probably halfway back to the stables by now.

And Ismena's laughter rings through the trees.

I never wanted to win the prince's challenge, but rage boils through me. It's one thing to lose fairly, quite another to have someone cheat you of the chance.

And I have a bridle. This game's not over yet.

Looking up, I focus on the shadows beneath the canopy, and a smile stretches over my lips. This is an old, dark forest. It was practically made for me.

I Sift into the shadows, moving faster than the swiftest horse.

Nothing moves faster than light, and I am merely the absence of it.

Ahead of me, the hounds are baying in excitement. A horn sounds, echoing through the trees. It's dark in the shadows, and occasionally I catch glimpses of gold embroidery or flashing gemstones as I pass one of the young princesses.

I Sift from tree to tree, until I'm finally ahead of them. Below me, darkhounds scramble around a narrow valley, sniffing and baying.

Forging back into mortal form, I run along the bridge of a tree limb, as nimble as a squirrel.

The unicorn snorts in front of me, cornered in a rocky canyon snarled with brambles. Dapples of light gleam on its pale coat, and its mane is long and tangled. A horn juts from between its eyes, as dull as unpolished marble. There's a certain sense of wildness that emanates from it that almost makes me catch my breath.

That anyone could think to hunt it down for its horn makes me feel ill. This is a creature to worship, to cherish. It belongs here in the wild, not harnessed by any man's hand.

"Easy," I whisper, as I slip from tree limb to tree limb until I'm on the ground.

The creature snorts, its eyes flashing their whites.

That horn lowers in my direction, and suddenly I'm staring directly at a two-foot-long weapon that could impale me.

"I'm not here to cause trouble, old friend," I murmur, holding up a hand. "I just want to borrow you for a few hours."

It could escape, but to do so would mean forcing its way through those inch-long thorns. Nobody else has arrived, which means it's not quite panicked enough to risk it, though I expect it will bolt the second they do. And while it's clearly uncertain of my intentions, it's not precisely afraid.

I have this one chance.

Easing the bridle forward, I watch its hindquarters tense. Nostrils flare, as if it's scenting the hair.

"See?" I take a slow step forward. "I mean you no harm. And while this might not have come from my head, you can smell the innocence on it, can't you?"

Another slow, stealthy step.

The unicorn's muzzle trembles.

I can't believe I'm about to touch it.

Then my fingers are stroking down that velvety muzzle.

"Aren't you a beautiful boy?" I whisper.

Horns blare.

The unicorn snorts and dances away from me. Suddenly, it's rushing at me, and I'm two seconds away from being trampled when I Sift.

Just a second.

Just a moment in the shadows.

Then I'm locking a fist in its tangled mane and sweeping onto its broad back. The thought occurs: I am riding a fucking unicorn.

And then it goes ballistic beneath me.

A furious, spine-bending rage that threatens to jettison me straight into the thorns. I've never felt such uncontained fury, such rage. Knotting my hands in its mane, I'm forced to ride it out, knees and thighs squeezing around its barrel-like chest.

Fuck. The bridle!

I swiftly lean forward to loop it over the creature's horn. It's barely tangled around the unicorn's muzzle, but the second the virgin's hair touches its flesh, it calms.

"That's it, big fellow." I can hear other horses crashing through the trees now. We're about to have company, and a new thought occurs.

Why not have some fun?

There's only one way into this trap, after all.

I wheel the unicorn around, and to my delight, Princess Ismena is the first to come crashing through the glade.

She screams as we charge, forced to blunder sideways. I catch a glimpse of her face as I bow mockingly. Then we're past, and this time, it's my turn to lead the hunt.

7

"And here I thought you were uninterested in winning my company," Prince Keir murmurs with the faintest of smiles as he shows me to my seat.

We're at the top of the tallest tower in the castle, overlooking the sea far below.

Someone's set up a small table with a pair of chairs, and candles weep fat globules of wax on every surface. If I close my eyes and focus, I can hear the crashing of the surf.

"I am... uncertain, as I said. But I cannot abide losing, either."

Especially not to spoiled princesses.

"Ah." He eases my chair in as I sit. "A conundrum indeed. Now you're trapped with me for the next few hours."

"At least the view is nice." There's a moment of silence, and my gaze shoots to his, recognizing the faint smirk there. "I meant—"

"I know." He leans back in the chair, one wrist resting on his propped-up knee. "No woman can resist me."

I roll my eyes. "This one can."

"You do wonders for my ego."

"I'm sure you're more than capable of stroking it yourself."

Oh, gods. My mouth just won't stop. He laughs as I bury my face in my hands. "Are we still talking about my ego?"

"*Yes.*"

"Forgive me for noticing, but for a court-raised lady, you're shockingly inept at flirtation and social niceties."

"Greenslieves is somewhat lacking in courtiers," I say weakly. And the lands of the Forbidden even more so. "To further show my ineptness, may I ask you a question?"

The prince pops the cork on the bottle of elderberry wine and gives me a magnanimous nod. "You may. Whether I answer it or not is up to me."

"Why now?" I demand, resting both elbows on the table as he fills my glass. "You've spent three thousand years locked away in this Other World, only to suddenly decide to Summon a bride? I won't believe three thousand is your lucky number. And if you were merely interested in scratching an itch, I'm sure there's an abundance of nubile fae women in this world."

"A costly answer. How about I trade you? A secret for a secret?"

It could be dangerous.

The fae cannot lie. While my wraithen half saves me from being held to the truth, if Keir is given any reason to suspect I'm not telling it, then the results could be deadly.

"As long as you go first," I murmur, sipping the wine.

"There's that issue of trust again."

"Something we both share," I point out.

He leans back in the chair, oozing grace. "I'm not searching for a bride. I'm searching for my mate."

I nearly spit the wine across the table.

The Great Goddess of the Cauldron gifted her fae children with both a promise—and a curse. For every fae, there's another soul out there, waiting to be joined to theirs. A truemate. Another half.

Fae males are offered a glimpse of their future mate during their adult rites. A spelled object will show them a clue of their mate's identity if the Goddess of the Cauldron is kind enough. It may take a century—or dozens—to find their other half, but fae males are territorial and possessive, and they never stop looking.

But if the other half of your soul dies, then you'll spend eternity wandering and feeling restless.

As I hack and cough, I can't help noticing the amused smile he fails to hide. He's enjoying this lack of decorum— or perhaps, enjoying the fact he's shocked me.

"Mother of Mercy," I mutter, burying my face in the napkin. "You're serious?"

"I looked into the Cauldron many, many years ago, and while I wasn't shown her face, I was shown the constellations in the sky that would herald her appearance." He points to the comet on the horizon. "The time is nigh. I have waited thousands of years for this moment."

"And now you need to work out which one of us it is."

"I had my seneschal consult the seer. Certain bloodlines showed promise according to the astrological signs of their births."

Thank the Goddess.

My birth date won't be on that list.

"Don't breathe a word of that to the others, or there'll be more blood in the hallways." To be wed to this dark lord offers a wealth of opportunities, but to realize you could be his mate? "Unless... unless someone has already started. You don't think the Wyrdwolf had anything to do with this?"

His smile fades. "Let us talk of other things tonight. Let my guards deal with the nightmare."

"In other words, don't worry my pretty little head?"

"Is it pretty?" He savors his wine, his golden eyes watching me. "I hadn't noticed."

"That's because it's up here," I reply, pointing to my face. "And you've been staring at other parts of me tonight."

Keir's eyes light up. "One can hardly fail to notice. I thought I was supposed to stare?"

I tug at my neckline with a growl. The gauzy lace is the color of seafoam and almost as insubstantial. I have to admit it stole my breath when Soraya hauled it out of the trunk, but the neckline dips between my breasts, meeting right at my sternum, where a knot of golden braid hugs my ribs. I've seen less skin at a fleshmongers. "It wasn't my idea, all right? This was what... the maids packed for me."

"Your *maids* have exquisite taste."

This isn't how the night's supposed to go. I was supposed to throw him off the scent after last night. Be rude, perhaps a little surly. But it's so easy to slip into a faintly flirtatious undertone with him.

Perhaps that's because I'm not the only one who's showing more skin than expected.

Keir has a liking for flowing robes that leave his chest and stomach bare. This one is midnight blue silk, and it highlights every golden inch of his skin. The fae are beautiful, and there's no dearth of exquisite males in the Alliance courts, but there's something unearthly about him that captures the eye—and my breath. Something a little dangerous.

"And you?" he murmurs, as the servants bring forth a series of silver-domed platters. "You claim you're only here to fulfill your father's promise, and have no interest in being chosen unless you're certain of my heart. Unless... there's already a claim upon yours?"

"No claim."

"But you're still wary."

"Would you believe it's you?" I reply as a half dozen plates are set on the tables between us. "Or is that simply impossible for a male of your... esteem?"

"It's a pity," he replies. "Because you certainly entertain me. And no, I won't believe it's me. You've never met me before this Summons. You have no reason to dislike me."

"Perhaps I simply don't enjoy having my chain jerked." There's some truth to the words. "Coming here wasn't my idea. The idea of debasing myself at your feet simply so you'll notice me leaves a bad taste in my mouth. Then there's the fact there are over twenty females here, baying for your attention, and you're certainly not discouraging it."

"How else am I to find the right one?"

"You were going to kiss me last night, weren't you? Before the screaming started. Tell me: How many of the other princesses are you planning to kiss?"

"As many as it takes," he admits. "It's how a male knows."

I stare past him at the stars. "I know the idea is irresistible, that there's someone out there who was made just for you. But how will your mate feel when she knows you've been flirting and kissing other women just to find her?"

"You have a curious view of fae nature."

My cheeks flush. It's true. The fae are amorous, and share their affections with many. Sometimes at once. I've never met a prudish fae, or one who feels uncomfortable in their skin.

Even in the Court of Shadows, debauchery is the name of the game. I've been witness to more orgies than I could have deemed possible.

But something about the concept strikes me as wrong.

"Perhaps Greenslieves is more backwater than I thought," I say softly, turning my attention to the food. "This looks lovely."

"I thought that if you didn't enjoy the company, you'd at least enjoy dinner." He's watching me again, as if making a dozen silent assumptions.

As I ladle a small amount of shellfish onto my plate and drizzle it with sauce, I cannot help thinking the opposite.

The company itself is quite intriguing.

And it cannot afford to be.

"So?" Soraya demands as soon as I'm back in my chambers. "Have you learned anything from the prince?"

"Yes." I slip out of my gown and tug on the nondescript black leathers I usually wear on a job. "I applied the thumb-screws and he told me exactly where the Dragon's Heart is. Easiest job I've ever been on."

She stares at me flatly. "We're wasting time."

"You may have noticed the legions of guards out and about today," I drawl, sliding half a dozen knives into various sheaths about my body. "If we knew where the Heart was, it might be a good opportunity to use the distraction to steal it. But we don't. Which means we both need to keep our heads low. I don't tell you how to assassinate someone. Don't tell me how to do my job. Father gave me the lead on this. I don't particularly want to have to tell him you bungled it through sheer impatience."

She flops on the bed with a snarl. "We're so close. Don't you want your freedom?"

Every damned day. "Of course I do."

But he's only offered it to one of us.

A nervous itch trickles down my spine. I wasn't overly bothered at having Soraya at my back, but the thought she might be here for her own purposes is a little concerning. Maybe I'll have to watch her a little more closely once we discover where the relic is. "How was your day? Find the treasury?"

"It's that enormous building across the rose gardens. They've got crews of twelve guarding it. I pretended to flirt with one of the guards. Didn't even have to kill anyone."

"That's a first."

Her eyes flash fire. "I'm saving my knife for later. If anyone gets in my way, I'll make it nice and bloody."

I don't say it, but I know my name is on that list.

"Then let's go examine the treasury," I murmur, turning toward the door. "Twelve guards? That doesn't seem like enough to guard something precious."

"That's because you haven't seen them yet," she replies. "I didn't say they were fae."

8

S oraya's right.

Twelve guards aren't enough for a treasury that houses one of your most valuable relics.

Unless they're beastkin sentries.

Half-animal, half-fae, I thought they were all exiled during the wars, but they're the actual living remnants of the Unseelie court. Some wear horns and goats legs, others have the head and teeth of a jungle cat set atop a muscular human torso, another looks like he wears the head of a bull.

"Cauldron's piss," I curse under my breath, as we scan the building. "Getting past is going to be a nightmare."

They'll smell me for sure.

"But you're the best for this job," Soraya protests mockingly. "I'm sure you won't *bungle* it."

Sisters. You can never trust them to return various aspects of your wardrobe, but when it comes to repeating the words you threw in their face, their memories are impeccable.

"I'm not going to bungle it." I squat in the shadows as I consider the task. I'm going to have to move swiftly, even as I

Sift. And hope there's no more beastkin inside. "Wish me luck."

"I'm sure you won't need it," she replies with an evil smile.

Fine. I draw the half-mask that's slung around my neck up over my nose and mouth, and haul my cloak over my hair. "If I get caught, then I'm throwing you to the wolves."

"Wouldn't expect anything else," she replies, though there's a hint of fondness there.

And as I Sift, I almost catch the faintly whispered, "*Good luck,*" that leaves her lips.

The enormous columns that ring the treasury doors are full of shadows. I land with a blink, and then I'm reaching for the thin line of shadows beneath the main doors before the nearest guard can even turn his head. The hardest part about Sifting is that you can only travel as far as you can directly see.

Inside.

Blink. More columns, more guards, more shadows.

Blink. Blink. Blink.

I finally find a ledge to rest upon as I blur back into mortal form. Sifting can be tiring, and it's hard to see your surroundings when you're veiled in shadows. From up here, I get a bird's eye view of the treasury's inner chambers.

The inside of the building is lit with softly glowing fey lanterns. I expected piles of riches, ancient treasures and artifacts, or perhaps a long line of vaults where all Prince Keir's precious little baubles are locked away.

It's just a single enormous hall—which is fucking empty.

What mockery is this? I nearly explode in frustration, but then something catches my eye.

Set right in the middle of the room is an enormous mirror. I Sift across the floor, barely daring to alight upon it before I'm gone again. But no alarms ring through the building at the touch of my foot, no wards suddenly cascade down, trapping me....

I try again.

And one last time, just to test the security surrounding the object.

Nothing.

The light from the lanterns barely reaches the dark mirror. Its surface is a sheen of pure obsidian.

A strange, possibly cursed object, locked away by itself in a heavily guarded building. Oh no, this isn't suspicious at all.

It's surrounded by a gilt-edged frame with ancient runes carved in it. I circle it curiously. Dark mirror.... Why does this sound familiar?

There are spelled mirrors that can show you your heart's desire or your worst nightmare. Mirrors that can tell you how beautiful you are. Mirrors that can show you your enemy's most dangerous weakness.

But which one is this?

I study the runes. The symbol of *aarwain* means desire. But *yaarwen* suggests to beware.

And *ruh* means to see.

But to see what?

"Show me the Dragon's Heart," I whisper hopefully. "Show me where it is."

The mirror's opaque surface transforms, and suddenly I'm staring at an image of Prince Keir. He leans over a basin of water, his chest bare as he scrubs at the stubble on his jaw. No male should look like such utter perfection, and I can't help noticing the way the towel wrapped around his waist dips dangerously low.

Stupid fucking mirror. I push away from it.

But then the urge to look back is almost dangerously compelling. I'm not intending to do anything of the kind. I need to get out of here.

But the next thing I know, I'm standing back in front of the mirror.

"Show me my soul-trap."

A faint silvery light appears, deep in the heart of the mirror. It slowly swims closer, that amorphous sliver of my soul trapped behind spelled crystal. My father wears it around his throat, but his features are a blur. I haven't asked to see him, only the soul-trap, so that's all it shows me.

I have no way of knowing how long I stand there. I'm vaguely aware of the flickering of fey lanterns. Of the ache of my legs, locked into place.

But all I can see is my truest desire.

Sweat beads on my forehead as I struggle to break the mirror lock. I know what this is now. The mirror's the bait. A Dark Object spelled to trap anyone who glances into it, until the guards do their next rotation. It will show you anything you want to see. All you have to do is look into it.

Just don't expect to escape it.

Cauldron's piss.

How am I going to get out of here when I can't even look away?

"Show me the Dragon's Heart," I repeat, my fingernails cutting into my palms.

Once again, Prince Keir comes into view. He's slinking toward a wide, tiled bath that looks somewhat akin to the one off my chambers. Steam curls off the water, and he's lost the towel.

Help. I do not need to know that.

But something else captures my attention.

The mirror blurs the edges of the view, thank the

Goddess, or I'd be staring right at the Prince of Dreams's most valuable possession.

Instead, the view is focused on his chest. Granted, it's a lovely chest, but the charm that lies against his sun-kissed skin winks in the light, and my breath catches. Maybe the mirror wasn't lying with that first image.

Maybe it's not showing me Keir, after all?

It's a primitive piece of jewelry, and I've seen him wearing it before. Carved in the shape of a claw, it's the length of my index finger and made of solid gold.

Amongst all the marble and gems that exists in this court, it fades into insignificance.

But where else does one hide a valuable relic?

Right in plain sight.

Slipping it off Keir's neck without him noticing its loss is significantly more difficult than breaking into a treasury. This is the cursed Prince of Dreams, after all. But now I know why there's been no hint of magical relics in his palace or in the treasury.

Now I know where it is.

I just need to break the mirror lock.

Easier said than done.

I know what the runes say now: *Beware those who look into the glass, for your true desire will trap you.*

Somehow I need to break the chain.

"Show me the creature who killed Lady Altrea."

The mirror resists. It wants to offer me fortunes and futures. It wants to trap me with gold and gems and hints of Prince Keir's bare flesh.

Don't I want to see my mother?

Don't I want to see my fae relatives?

It could show me.

All I have to do is ask.

The thoughts are not my own, and the second I even think about my mother, I see a face forming in the heart of the mirror's black depths. A face I cannot afford to see, because then I'll never be able to look away.

"Show me the creature," I almost sob.

The mirror offers me a glimpse of the dining hall last night, but I can sense its reluctance. I was expecting to see the Wyrdwolf, but then... that's not what I asked.

My breath catches as I see half a dozen of the princesses; Altrea, Narcissa, Calliope, Ismena, and two other girls I barely recognize.

"*Go home,*" Princess Ismena sneers at one of the girls. "*You don't belong here. Neither of your bloodlines could even dream of tempting the prince.*"

"*Perhaps he's not concerned with our bloodlines,*" one of the princesses replies bravely. Everly, I think. We've spoken once, but not again.

Ismena steps forward, her face mottled with ugliness. "*Don't make me do something I'll regret. Your little 'secret' is safe from me. For now. But I think the prince might be quite interested in the taint in your blood.*"

"*Ismena,*" Altrea murmurs, catching her arm. "*That's enough, isn't it?*"

"*Oh, let her continue,*" Calliope says, drawing Everly protectively closer. "*The prince is no fool. He'll see what she is. All the precious bloodlines in the world can't hide bad breeding.*"

"You *speak* of breeding?" Ismena sneers. "*You? I daresay if we check beneath your dress we'll find a tail. You're Unseelie scum.*"

"*It's not my tail you should be worried about,*" Calliope replies heatedly.

I want to see more.

I want to see if my suspicion is correct: one of these precious princesses summoned the creature to kill Altrea.

But the mirror wants me to linger. Even now it leaps ahead eagerly.

And I can hear voices behind me.

Steps coming closer.

How long have I been standing here?

Break the trap, damn you.

I want to see who Altrea's murderer is, and so the lock holds its grip on me. I need to see something I *don't* ever want to remember.

"Show me the last night in the training camps. Show me Soraya's betrayal."

There. That ought to do the trick.

The mirror goes dark, rebelling. But it cannot fight its nature.

Two figures emerge from the barren wastelands of the mountaintop. It's a simple challenge to pass our training and go on to the challenger rounds. Every trainee had three days to make it to the top of Shadowfang, the mountain that dwarfs all others.

If you weren't among the first five, then you were culled.

We were among the best, two of the handful that could almost pass as fae. Two of Father's favorites. From the moment I was thrown into the training camps and found my dark-hearted sister, we'd been inseparable. Soraya cried for the first month, as she'd only recently been torn from her mother, and I'd spent every night curled up in the rough blankets she'd been given, my arms around her.

"*Don't cry,*" I'd whispered. "*I lost my mother too. But we can be sisters.*"

But the years had passed.

And I hadn't foreseen the hungry look in her eyes.

Only one could be crowned champion.

Only one could serve at the Wraith King's right hand.

In the mirror, I reach for her hand, knowing another of the candidates is right on my heels, his knife gripped between his teeth. Together we'd fought our way up the mountain, half-blinded by ice and snow, facing an entire squad of bastards intending to tear us down.

Soraya squats above me on the ledge, our hands clasping as she tries to haul me up. Two of my ribs were broken defending her from an unforeseen attack, and the cold has wrought its damage on me. I need every ounce of help I can get.

"*Hurry!*" I cry as Torrin reaches for my boot.

We know three candidates have already made it.

Only two more will get a chance.

Torrin grabs at my ankle, and his additional weight almost hauls Soraya over the edge. I scream as torn muscles burn. Soraya's thigh muscles flex and strain, and she grinds her teeth together as I dangle precariously.

There's another pair of candidates to our left, scaling the cliff face determinedly. They're almost neck and neck with us.

"*Kick him off!*" she screams.

"*Don't let me go!*"

But she's glancing across, judging the distance. Knowing they're going to beat her to the top if she's not careful.

And I relive every moment of it as I watch.

"*I'm sorry,*" she whispers, meeting my eyes. "*I don't want to die.*"

"*We could fight together. We could flee. We promised we'd always have each other's backs!*"

But she lets me go.

The mirror's hold on me shatters, and the second I tear my eyes from its surface, I Sift away.

None too soon.

The guards burst in, seemingly alerted somehow to my presence.

But I don't linger to see if they're disappointed to find the room empty.

～

"NOTHING?" Soraya demands as I reappear at her side.

Seeing the moment of her betrayal has shaken me all over again, but I realized something too. I missed her. I missed the little girl who shared my bed on bad nights, where we'd whisper our hopes and dreams and she'd tell me about the mother she could barely remember. I miss the training partner who sparred with me every day and laughed with me about some of the other boys in the camp. And I missed the girl who'd splash me in the face in the hot baths when I teased her about a certain boy in particular.

That doesn't mean I trust her.

"It wasn't there. But now I know where it is."

"Where?" Her eyes light up.

I merely smile. "Maybe it's time for Lady Merisel to seduce a prince?"

She rolls her eyes. "Has he got it with him, or are you merely trying to get him naked?"

"Both?"

And a hint of a smile crosses her mouth, before she slaps me across the back of the head. "Mind on the job, Zemira. We're running out of time."

～

THERE'S an uproar in the palace, and I swiftly change into my gown again, trying to hide my late-night sojourn.

Soraya gives me a look. "What's going on?"

"I'll find out."

"If you don't come back, should I check the prince's bed?" she calls as I slip from the room.

Scurrying through the halls, I'm drawn to the sounds of sobbing, and find most of the prince-hunting party near the library.

Prince Keir is there, trying to send them all away.

But it's too late.

We've all seen what he's looking at. What he's trying to hide from view. The smooth marble walls are no longer unblemished. It takes me a moment to realize what I'm looking at: the drape of a skirt spilling from within the marble; a bloodred ruby shattered on the floor; and a pair of hands sticking out of the stone, as if trying to claw for help.

I stare at those hands, at the body clearly entombed in the marble.

"So ends Narcissa's hunt," Calliope murmurs at my side.

I startle.

"Narcissa?"

"Don't you recognize the rings on her fingers?" Calliope drawls. Her gaze slides to where Ismena is only just making an appearance.

"What's going on?" the Princess of Storms demands. "What's all this noise?" She finally sees the hands, and her mouth drops open. "What happened?"

"It seems one by one, princesses are going missing," Calliope tells her coldly. "Or dying. Where were you tonight?"

"In my bedchambers," Ismena replies, arching one cool brow. "Dinner disagreed with me."

"Can anyone confirm your whereabouts?" Calliope demands.

"Why? Are you asking if anyone was with me?" Ismena glances at the prince as if she's got something to hide. "Of course not. I was alone. The only one who saw me was my maid."

"And we all know where her loyalties lie."

"If you're calling me a liar, then say it," Ismena hisses, balling her fists at her sides.

"That's enough," snarls the prince.

Both females step apart, though Ismena's hot glare promises retaliation for this.

"Return to your chambers, all of you," Prince Keir says. "I shall have guards posted at your doors. If you are seen outside your chambers, it shall be assumed you know more about this state of affairs than it seems."

His gaze slides over me, as if he wants to speak to me but does not dare.

I try not to look at the golden claw hanging from his throat.

There shall be no seduction tonight.

I shoot what is left of Narcissa one last look as I slink back to my rooms with the rest of the girls.

I can't help thinking about what I saw in the mirror tonight. Despite her initial "shock," Ismena has recovered well and is muttering horrible things about Calliope that everybody can hear.

"Better watch your back," I murmur as Calliope pauses by her door. "Ismena doesn't seem too fond of you right now."

"Is she ever fond of anyone?" Calliope muses, watching the other princesses go.

"I thought... I thought she was friendly with Narcissa." The choice of victim confuses me.

"Narcissa won a picnic with the prince tomorrow," Calliope replies.

It startles me. "She did?"

"I forget, you weren't there tonight when we were swimming in the pools in the rose garden." Calliope gives me a steady look, and I hope she's not thinking I had anything to do with this.

"There's only so much nastiness I can handle."

Calliope takes a breath. Then pauses. "You know... you're not like the others."

"I hope you mean that as a compliment."

She smiles. "I do. I didn't think I'd like anyone here, but you remind me of myself. I've been so alone for so long now, that I didn't think I missed having a friend." She steps forward and impulsively hugs me. "Be careful. The other girls think you're the competition."

And I don't want to end up like poor Narcissa or Altrea.

"I will be," I promise as she steps back. "If Ismena plans to come after me, then she'd better bring her best knives." I flash a smile. "I'm no easy target."

9

I plead a headache the next day as the prince and his cohort of ass-kissers ride out for another afternoon of bride hunting. After last night, I don't have the stomach for it.

He doesn't quite look disappointed when I say I'm staying, though he does smile and murmur, "Avoiding me again?"

To which I roll my eyes. "Only you would think I've feigned a headache to avoid your company."

"I don't know *what* gives me that idea."

Caught.

"If you're feeling better tonight, perhaps you might care to play a game of Redcap with me in my rooms?"

It's the perfect opportunity. I don't know why I hesitate. "Perhaps. If I feel better."

He nods and mounts up, but his hot eyes watch me as he wheels his black stallion out the gate.

I waste no time. Despite the invitation—or perhaps because of it—I decide it's my only chance to search the prince's rooms. He doesn't always wear the claw, though try as I might, I couldn't see whether he was wearing it beneath his shirt when he left.

Afternoon sunlight is when I'm at my worst, but it's a simple matter to Sift into his bedchambers.

Not quite so simple to find what I'm looking for.

There's no sign of the relic. He must be wearing it, which means I must face him again.

Tonight.

I glance at his bed. I joked about it with Soraya, but the idea of stealing a kiss from the prince just so I can slip the relic from around his throat makes my stomach roil. We've barely had any time together—I *have* been avoiding him of late—but I know his thoughts on betrayal.

And worse, I know the feel of it.

I don't want to do this.

It was one thing to filch Angmar's precious trident. The king is Blessed through and through and makes Ismena look like a kindly soul. I enjoyed stealing it, truth be told.

But Prince Keir has been kind. He's solicitous, charming, protective... and while he's making a pretense of playing the game, I know the deaths of the two princesses have bothered him greatly.

I won't pretend he's not dangerous. It's there in every step he takes, every flicker of those hot gold eyes. The man's a predator who exists at the top of the food chain. Cross him, and I'm sure he'll rain his wrath down upon you.

But he's not cruel.

And he doesn't deserve this.

Think of the soul-trap. Think of freedom. Think of everything you can do when you're no longer beholden to the Wraith King.

It doesn't help.

Because once I'm free, what then?

I have nowhere to go. I have no one to go to.

And every time I look in the mirror, I'll know my freedom came at the cost of his trust.

It makes me feel dirty.

THAT NIGHT, every eye is on Ismena, and she knows it. There's an air of nervousness around the dining room.

Nobody goes anywhere alone—even to the washroom— and dinner conversation is subdued. There's no sign of Prince Keir.

Probably a good thing, for I haven't yet resolved my feelings in regards to tonight's invitation.

If I don't go to his rooms, I'll probably never get another invitation.

If I do, then I'll destroy the hint of... something... that lingers between us.

"Well, since the company is so subdued tonight, I think I might just retire." Ismena makes a grand show of pushing her chair back.

Over a dozen eyes watch her.

And she's clearly a little bothered by the fact no one says anything.

She recovers well. "I guess I'll see you all in the morning. Or whoever makes it through until dawn."

Nasty words, but as she leaves, I realize her shoulders are squared and her fingers curl into the fabric of her skirts, as if she can practically feel the daggers lobbed at her back.

Or as if she's scared.

Something has been bothering me about the entire ordeal.

Ismena's a typical Blessed bitch, quite content to tear others to shreds when she's one of the group, but now that she stands alone she's almost scared. She's not the type to face a fight without someone at her back. A coward through and through, who only gains her claws in company.

But now the little coterie she formed on the first day has vanished. Altrea and Narcissa were her closest allies, and the other girl who hovered in their shadows—Louella of Goldenrod—is suddenly pretending Ismena has the pox.

Altrea and Narcissa. Why were they the first to fall?

Why would Ismena kill *them*?

Narcissa may have won a private picnic with the prince, but he's made it clear he's unimpressed with their nasty jibes.

As Calliope said, the other girls see me as the competition, but although the Wyrdwolf attacked me the other night, I wasn't the target.

And Ismena hates me.

If she had anything to do with this, I would have been the first victim and Narcissa and Altera would have cheered her on.

I've been so distracted by the prince and Soraya, that I didn't even think it through.

With Ismena gone, the other princesses are also retiring.

A prickle of suspicion trickles down my spine.

The attacks have happened every night, and I cannot help but wonder if my suspicions are correct and I know who the next victim will be.

I make my escape politely and dart around the nearest massive column into the shadows there. She has a head start on me, but I can move quicker than she can.

Blurring from shadow to shadow, I soon catch a glimpse of Ismena, pausing in the hallway that leads to her room.

One of the sconces suddenly dies, right outside her

chambers. Ismena freezes. "Hello?" she calls softly. "Is anyone there?"

Why are there no guards in this section of the palace?

Another lamp abruptly plunges into darkness.

Sibilant laughter whispers through the hallway, and it doesn't sound as if it comes from any sort of fae throat.

"What's wrong?" whispers the voice. "Are you frightened, Ismena?"

Ismena staggers back a step, but she's whirling round, as if she's too afraid to flee. "Guards? Guards!"

"No one's coming to save you." There's a shadowy figure at the end of the hall, and it's suddenly rushing toward the princess. "You will die alone, and nobody will give a damn because nobody cares about you."

Ismena screams and finally turns to flee.

The cloaked figure is almost upon her, lifting a knife to plunge it into her back.

I Sift into the world again, slamming into the assassin. Rolling apart, we come onto hands and knees staring at each other as Ismena bolts to safety.

And then I blink.

I'd been unsure of which princess the assassin would be, but the woman staring back at me—

"Calliope?" What in the Cauldron's name?

There's a sharp, merciless edge to her face, as if her glamour's slipped. Eyes glowing molten in the night, she bares her teeth. "Where did you come from?"

"What are you doing?" I demand, tension coiling through my body. But I already know the answer. "You killed Altrea and Narcissa."

"They deserved it."

"They were harmless," I snap. "All teeth and claws, but no bite."

She straightens with a dangerous grace, and so do I. I can't help thinking of poor Narcissa's hands, forever reaching through that wall. What a horrible way to die.

"If it had been you who met my nightmares, do you think either of *them* would have shed a tear, worm?" she demands.

"It's just a name," I reply. "Why care what someone hateful calls you? Once this was over, I'd never have given them another thought. They were stupid and wretched and *unimportant*."

And perhaps they knew it, deep in their hearts.

Perhaps it's the sense of such self-doubt that causes petty princesses to try and tear each other down.

"Why?" I whisper.

None of this makes any sense, for Calliope's never shown any great interest in stealing the prince for herself.

And she was the one who told me *I* was the competition.

Why kill them if they're no threat to her? Why... is she even here if she has no interest in the prince's hand in marriage?

"I am born of greatness. And I shall not suffer the likes of them looking down their noses at me." Calliope seems to grow taller. "They are nothing to me. They ought to have groveled. Instead, they earned their fate when they sneered."

Greatness? What is wrong with her? "Why are your eyes glowing?" I whisper.

"Because it's waking," she whispers, shadows stretching out behind her like wings.

"What's waking?"

"You don't want to find out. Get out of here. I don't want to have to hurt you. You have done me some kindness these past few days. I remember."

"But the other princesses are fair game?"

"The other princesses are merely distraction." She draws another knife. "I'm not here for them. Nor am I here for you. If you get out of my way, I won't kill you."

"You're here for Keir." He'd said he thought someone had twisted the Other World to their magic, but this makes no sense. "You plan to kill him? Why?"

"Because I need to eat his heart."

Of all the things I expected her to say.... "Old lover? Killed your father? Owes your people a debt he won't repay?"

"This is not revenge," she croons, caressing the knife in her hand.

I step back, watching it carefully. "I thought you didn't have a taste for meat." She's picked at every meal here, eating only that which comes from the ground or the forest.

"This is not about flesh."

With each step closer, Calliope's eyes seem just a little more inhuman. I once thought them akin to an eagle's eyes, but now I'm not so sure. I've seen that amber glow before, as if something primordial looks back at me. Every instinct I own is telling me to flee, but I can't help thinking of the prince.

"The blood of ancient queens runs through my veins," Calliope croons. "I can feel it waking in me, but I'm not strong enough. Not yet. I can't access the reservoir of power within me. I can't Awaken. I need his heart to bloom."

"Easy now, caterpillar. Eating a fae heart is only going to give you indigestion. Especially this one."

If not a fatal sword in the guts. She's trying to bite off more than she can chew.

"Haven't you realized what you're dabbling with yet?" she sneers. "You think the prince is fae?"

"What do *you* think he is?"

"I think he's a myth. I think he's masked himself very carefully over the years so no one suspects the truth. He's the key to my transformation. The power in his heart will Awaken me."

Oh, shit. Someone's been eating the fuzzy mushrooms. "You're not making any sense."

"Why don't you ask him what happened to the dragons? I've spent years tracking down old stories. They say they slumber. They say they turned to stone. All that power, and Queen Mab brought them to their knees. Have you never wondered how?"

"Not... really." If I can keep her talking, then hopefully Keir or Soraya will find me.

"Queen Mab went to the King of the Dragons and proposed a truce between their peoples, forged with a marriage. There was a child," she whispers, "born of both races."

I've never heard this story.

"A daughter who held the power of the stars in her blood, though the dragon was trapped within her. Her father beheld what she was to become and called her abomination, but the Princess Igrainne turned all of that immense power upon him and he fell. Together, she and Mab cut his heart from his chest, and the princess consumed it. With his power combined with her own, she finally had the ability to become what she was meant to be.

"More powerful than a dragon. Fierce and furious and hungry. One heart was not enough. She became afflicted with the need to consume more, and when the dragon race tried to take revenge for their fallen leader, she became their worst nightmare."

"I've never heard of Princess Igrainne."

"You wouldn't," Calliope says bitterly. "The dragons

turned to the gods to forge the Cauldron and use it against her. They trapped her in her mortal form, draining the power she'd stolen and filling the Cauldron with it. Igrainne had to flee, a mere shadow of herself. In return, the dragons were forced to honor their pact with the gods. They could no longer walk the world as primordial beings. They had to give up most of their power so it would not lure the princess from the shadows, for she hungered still. Until she drew her last breath, she would always crave a return to power. And then they buried all talk of her name. They choked her in nothingness and killed those who knew the story. Her memory is lost to the world, but her legacy lives on in the line of children she birthed. In me. I've felt it whispering through my veins ever since I was born."

And now she thinks consuming Prince Keir's heart will somehow transform her.

"Dragons don't exist anymore," I say. "They sleep." It's a lovely story, but if it were true, wouldn't I have heard it? No matter how hard you try, you cannot completely bury a rumor. There'd have been some mention of this Princess Igrainne in the history books.

"They don't all sleep," she hisses. "My mother told me that story at her knee. Every night, she would remind me of who I was, and what I was to become. The Cauldron—"

"The Cauldron was a gift from the Goddess."

"You lie!" Calliope lashes out with her blade, and I leap back as it cuts through the air where my abdomen was two seconds ago.

We stare at each other.

So this is the way it's to be.

"I should have killed you the first night," she says, her eyes lighting up with insane fury. "You don't understand.

You *are* a worm. A pathetic, lying wretch of a worm. I thought we could be friends."

She lunges toward me with the dagger. I block her blow, propelling the blade past my nose and snapping a flat palm up into her elbow. Calliope screams, but then she's lashing backward with the blade, a weak blow, but a dangerous one all the same.

"Friends don't kill other friends!" I yell, slapping aside her vicious jabs. The disengage has barely hurt her, and it should have dislocated her elbow.

"My mother warned me," she continues, as if I've said nothing at all. "No one will understand my greatness. They'll seek to trap me in this skin. They'll betray me and hunt me down if they realize what I am. I have to evolve."

"I think your mother should have gotten out more."

"Don't you speak her name." Calliope drives toward me, and this time I have no recourse but to grab her wrist and slam her sideways into one of the columns.

She screams in thwarted fury, and then her eyes glow with golden magic. "So be it!"

Something grabs hold of me from behind. I fly backward, slamming into another column, my head cracking on the marble. An explosion of pain slams through me and white drenches my vision.

I hit the floor, momentarily winded.

Movement blurs at me.

Years of reflexes save my life. I Sift out of the way, and Calliope's dagger drives into the floor.

Up to the hilt.

The Sift disorientates me further. I stagger against the column. It's no longer pure white. Blood mars its shiny surface. My blood.

Calliope looks up with murderous eyes. "Well now," she

whispers. "It seems I'm not the only one with a secret. Ismena was right. You're *not* a pureblood."

"Merisel!"

Prince Keir is running toward us, the flaming sword in his hands. And I suddenly realize he's calling *my* name. Or the name he knows me by.

Calliope's teeth bare in a dangerous smile. "And here is my heart. Here is my key to transformation."

She stands and wrenches at the air with her fist.

The columns start shuddering, tearing away from where they're rooted to the floor. Tiles tear free from the roof, shattering on the marble floor. Prince Keir glances up, and flicks his hand dismissively.

Abruptly, the hall straightens as though nothing ever happened. I'm too dizzy to wonder if I imagined it or not.

Shadows blur. Nightmares twist themselves into reality at the wave of her hand. A Wyrdwolf leaps at the prince, but he beheads it with a stroke, and its body splashes into an inky sludge on the floor behind him.

Calliope hisses in fury, and then she turns to me as if she knows she cannot overwhelm him.

"It's over," Prince Keir calls in a dangerously soft voice. "This is my world, and no matter your power, you will not wrest it from me."

But she's closer to me than he is.

"It's never over," she whispers and waves her hand at me.

Something grabs me from behind. Cold stone hauls me back toward the wall, and I'm reminded of Narcissa's fate. I can't Sift. I can't escape it. I scream as my body starts sinking into stone.

The last thing I see is a blur of golden light as the prince leaps toward her.

And then marble is closing over my face. It flows into my

mouth and nose, as if both liquid and solid all at once. I
can't scream anymore. I can't breathe.

I'm going to die here, trapped in the walls of the fucking
palace, and suddenly a riot of all the things I've never had a
chance to do ripples through my mind. I've never known
freedom. I've never known love. I've never had a chance to
escape the misery of the life I own.

Then everything is shifting.

The wall spits me out onto the hallway floor and I gasp
for breath, clinging to it for dear life. Thank the Goddess.
My mouth tastes dry and my heart is hammering, and what
in the Cauldron's name is wrong with my eyes?

"Merisel?" There's a knee in front of me, though floating
specks of white obliterate the center of my vision. "Are you
all right?"

Keir.

There's blood on his leather breeches, blood all over the
tiles. I see the body, but the white lights obliterate the worst
parts of it.

It's only when I turn my head that I realize he decapi-
tated her.

And I'm shaking as he draws me to my feet. Me, who's
faced the worst the Wraith King can throw at me.

But not this.

Not being buried alive in a wall.

I want to vomit.

"You're all right," Keir whispers, hauling me into his
arms. He cradles me against his chest, squeezing tightly, and
for a second I close my eyes, breathing in his scent. "I knew
the killer would strike tonight. The second Ismena came
screaming around the corner, I knew we had her, but I didn't
realize she had *you* in her sights. You're lucky you're still

alive." His voice roughens as he says it, and his hand strokes through my hair.

It feels... nice.

It feels like all the things I want and can't have.

"She was mad." I cannot shake the look in her eyes. "She thought that if she ate your heart she'd... transform. She thought herself a dragon."

"A dragon?" He draws back, his hands resting on my shoulders. "Are you all right, Merisel?" A tender thumb traces the blood dripping from my temple. "You hit your head."

"*She* hit my head."

Smashed it right into the nearest column.

"Here," he says, sweeping me up into his arms as if I'm some sort of damsel. "There's water and cloth in my rooms. That wound looks like it needs tending."

Nobody's ever carried me in their arms before. I grab his shirt, feeling awkward and precarious. If you cannot afford to stand on your own two feet, then you're in danger.

But that's the kind of thinking I grew up with.

This is Keir. He just saved my life.

I peer over his shoulder as his guards tend to the body. I didn't even realize they were there.

Calliope's eyes stare accusingly at me, her head several feet away from the rest of her.

Fuck it. If the prince wants to carry me, then he can.

Curse the training camps.

Curse my father.

And above all, curse the Dragon's Heart. For one hour of my life, I want to pretend I know nothing about it.

10

Prince Keir takes me to his rooms.

My mind's starting to clear as my pulse slowly comes back under control. I won't pretend I'm not a little dizzy still, but at least when he puts my feet on the ground I don't fall in a boneless puddle.

"Sit down before you fall down," he says.

"Not going to fall."

No matter what I must do.

"Stubborn," he says, but there's a hint of fondness to the words. Snapping his fingers, he summons a bowl of steaming water out of thin air and a pile of fresh linens.

Then his hand is planted firmly in the middle of my chest, and he pushes me gently onto the bed. I land and sink into the mattress as if it's made of the softest feathers.

"If you wanted me in your bed, you should have asked." Wait. Did I just say that? I touch my pounding head. I think I'm concussed.

"Yes, you most likely are," the prince replies, as if I spoke the thought out loud. "Here."

There's a gentle hand on my face, and heat brushing

against my head. It feels nice. It feels as though I can almost see again, as if my head's no longer throbbing.

"Mmm." I press his hand to my face like a cat seeking affection. "Good."

"That will heal some of the swelling inside your head." He wipes blood from my hair. "If I'd known all I had to do to get you alone again was knock you half unconscious, I might have tried it this morning."

"Ha." I rest my chin on my knee tiredly. "You might have my company, but I daresay the conversation is bound to be lacking."

"It's never lacking when it's with you." He dips the piece of linen in the water, and then dabs it against my wound. "You're always a challenge, and I know you're hiding something from me, but I like trying to work out what it is." He leans closer, his breath brushing against my lips. "You are a constant puzzle, and I cannot figure you out, Merisel."

Merisel.

How I'm coming to hate that name.

"You're a predator," I say flatly. "Of course you want to chase the one female you can't have."

"Can't I have her?" he muses. And then his thumb ripples down my cheek and brushes softly across my mouth. Back and forth, until I hold my breath, waiting to see what he'll do with it. "Because when she's being honest—like now—I know she wants me."

"There's your ego again," I whisper and shut my eyes.

Because I can't avoid the look in his own.

"Yes and no," he says. "I see it in your eyes every time you look at me. I see the war that's being waged. You fear being trapped by my offer. You fear you cannot trust it."

A bitter laugh escapes me, because he's so close to the truth....

And yet so far.

"You've been avoiding me ever since that night we dined," he whispers. "Why?"

Maybe I am still dizzy.

"Because I like you," I blurt. "And I shouldn't. It will ruin everything." I can barely get the words out. "I will ruin everything."

Keir cups my cheek in his hand, and my eyes shoot open only to find his face bare inches from my own, his eyes sparking gold as he leans closer to me. "Yes and no," he whispers. "It's still there."

I thought he was going to kiss me, but he merely brushes his lips to my temples. "I will wait until it's only a *yes*. I can be patient. I've been waiting for you for a very long time, Merisel."

My heart stops dead in its chest. I swear it does. I draw back sharply. "*What?*"

This can't be happening.

I push to my feet and stagger past him. "No. *No.*" This is precisely what I was trying to avoid. "You don't even know me."

"I know you are kind. I know you're strong, and a fighter, and you protect those who aren't. You knew Ismena was going to be attacked tonight, and despite your feelings for her, you tried to protect her," he says, seemingly amused by my panic. His voice roughens. "I know you are the one I want."

Which is precisely what I thought he was saying.

"Well, maybe you're not the one *I* want?"

Fear makes my voice harsh.

Keir stares at me.

"You barely know me," I whisper. "I'm not kind. I'm not.... I'm not *honest*. I can't be trusted. Not with your heart."

It's the closest I can get to warning him.

He smiles a little dangerously. "Yes and no. I will wait, Merisel. But you should know—I mean to have you, no matter how long I must wait. No matter how much you doubt me."

This is a nightmare.

He's like the mirror, offering me my greatest temptation, even as I feel the jaws of the trap closing around me.

"I'm sorry," I whisper, retreating toward the door. "I cannot be what you want me to be."

"Then I will wait."

The words follow me through the door as I slam it and press my back to it. This needs to end. Now. Tonight.

Before it's too late.

SORAYA ARCHES a brow the second she sees me. "You look like something the Cauldron just spat out."

I collapse back onto my bed with a groan. I feel like it too. Between the attack and Keir's sudden decision, I feel like I've been gut punched. "Try Calliope. Bitch was our crazy killer. Tried to bury me in a wall."

"Tried?"

"Keir cut off her head." I shudder. "And then he pulled me out of the wall. You're lucky you still have a sister."

Maybe it would have been for the best if he left me in there.

What am I going to do?

He flat-out stated his intentions to make me his wife.

His *princess*.

I was so out of sorts, I didn't even think of the fucking relic once. This is all turning to shit. The sooner we're out of here the better, but the second I think it, I know I'm in no hurry to pull off the job.

Because the second I do, I betray him.

My mouth tastes like ash.

Soraya kneels on the end of the bed and tugs at my right boot. "You shouldn't have trusted her."

"I didn't." It was a lesson learned from her all those years ago. My voice softens, "It doesn't mean I didn't like her."

"You didn't get a chance to steal the relic from the prince?"

"Don't. Not tonight. I'm tired and my head hurts." I sit up on the bed as she discards my boots behind her. Then she's helping with my gown, dragging the bloody remnants of it over my head. "The last thing I was thinking about was stealing the charm from around Keir's neck."

Soraya rubs my shoulders, and I can't stop them from softening. "Keir, is it?"

I shove her in the gut. "Is there anything to drink? My mouth tastes like a horse's ass."

Soraya's eyebrows rise as she turns to the decanter in the corner. "I wouldn't know what that tastes like."

"Liar. You've kissed enough donkeys in your time."

"But never their asses." She smiles as she pours me wine. "I used to leave that to you."

"I missed you," I admit, resting back on my hands. Maybe I hit my head harder than I thought? *Maybe I nearly died.* "I missed this."

Both of us working together, instead of at odds as it has been for the past ten years.

Soraya pauses, her dark eyes locking on me as I reach for the goblet in her hand. She resists slightly, but I arch a brow and take it from her with a smile.

"If only we didn't have to go back to Father," I muse,

sipping the wine. "Do you ever think of what it would be like to live in another court? To be free of him?"

"All the time," she whispers, but she still hasn't moved. Her face hardens. "This place is turning your head. Court of Dreams. Ha. There *is* no escape. Father owns us, body and soul."

I capture her hand, knowing she speaks of the past and what she suffered when she returned from her failed attempt to assassinate the Lord of Mistmark. King Raesh does not suffer failure lightly, but there'd been more to it, I was sure.

Especially when word came of the Lord of Mistmark's betrothal to a foreign princess last month. Soraya has been brooding ever since, though perhaps I'm the only one who can see it.

"He hasn't married her yet. There's still hope."

She tears her hand from mine. "I don't know what you speak of."

A lie, but perhaps our new truce doesn't extend so far.

"I think you do. You don't fail." I breathe the words into the air. "Father might believe you missed your mark, but I know you better. If you failed to kill the Lord of Mistmark, then there was a reason."

I know the girl who forged herself in the brutal training camps we'd endured in the Shadowfangs. The only way to survive was to be the best, and despite my efforts, not even I could come close to beating her at the games and bouts. There was a strength of will inside her that forged my sister into a cold, hard blade without mercy.

Soraya stares at me stonily.

"You won't speak his name," I continue, taking another drink of wine. "But you flinch when Father does. And you bore your punishment without a fight. You've never tolerated Father's abuse, but this time you did. I think we both know why. You didn't want Father to look too closely at *why* you failed. Did you love him?"

What does that feel like?

A flash of rage crosses her face, and she smashes the goblet from my hand. Wine soaks across the carpets, but I don't move. Not even when she strides to the window, glaring through it. "A half-born wraith bastard? I would not have dared."

"You should have dared."

After tonight, it's becoming more than clear that life is worth grasping by the hands. All those things I've never done, and I came close tonight to never having that chance again.

"And have Father crush my soul-trap in his fist?" She shoots me an angry look. "This is why you could never beat me. This is why I was the best. You hope. You dream. You have trust where there is none. You are weak. We must stand alone in this world or we will fall."

I push to my feet in protest... and somehow lose my balance.

Capturing myself against the bed, I try to shake off the sudden weakness in my knees. Must have been sitting too long. Maybe I'm still concussed. "Is it weak to dream of more?"

"Like what?" She turns on me, raking a disdainful look down me. "Like the handsome prince following you around like a fool? You think he's your answer? You think he would risk it all for you if he knew the truth of your ancestry? You think he would choose *you*?" A bitter laugh escapes her. "Gods, you're so trusting. You don't even truly know why Father sent me, do you? To be your *maid*?"

Once again I'm reminded we're not truly allies, no

matter how much I try. The room swims before my eyes, her words sounding as if they come from a great distance. This is no concussion.

"What did you do?" The wine looks like blood splashed across the floor, a sudden, ominous omen. Gods, my head is swimming. What was in the wine? "What did you give me?"

Soraya draws her knife. "It's not poison. You'll wake with the dawn, though you might regret it for a while. Night's Bloom has that effect, I'm told."

My feet go out from under me, pain slamming through my knees as I hit the ground. *Curse her. No!*

"You had your chance," Soraya continues, her voice echoing hollowly in my ears. "You failed to steal the charm. So I *will*, now you've told me where it is. No matter what I must do." There's a faint pause. "Love is a weakness. There is no place for it in this world. I loved you once, but we both would have died if I'd let it trap me."

And then she's gone.

Panic sweeps through me, like the wings of a swarm of moths.

My sister's deadly at the best of times. And she's no thief. She'll try and take the Heart by force, not misdirection. Prince Keir might be powerful, but he won't be expecting it.

I have to stop her.

Stumbling to the chamber pot, I thrust both fingers down my throat, forcing my gorge to rise. The wine comes up with a splash, in great, gasping heaves. Hopefully, it won't be too late.

When it's done, I fell to my hands and knees on the carpets, shaking all over and calling her every vile name under the sun.

I think of the prince and his story of betrayal. It's such a bitter fruit to taste, all the more so because only one you trust can strike so true.

He'll never forgive me for this, and the thought is enough to force me to my feet.

I stagger like a drunk fresh from a tavern.

Soraya is gone.

And so is the gown I was wearing.

11

Night's Bloom races through my veins as I stagger between shadows, desperate to make it toward Keir's chambers.

The enormous gilded doors are locked. Of course. Slamming my fists against them, I try to snatch at the wisp of shadows that lurk beneath them, but there's nothing there. Only a spill of light, as if someone's set a lantern near the door.

Soraya has accounted for my strengths.

But the bitch doesn't know me well enough.

It's been ten years since we fought each other in the training camps, and the girl she knew wasn't ruthless enough to face her sister and win *at all costs*. Something always held me back. Something always stopped me from striking a mortal blow that could have won me the title of champion and cost me a sister.

But there's nothing more inspiring than betrayal.

She wants to fight?

Fine.

Filmy curtains drift in the hallways, chased by the skitter

of wind through the arched windows. I haul myself through one of them and look down. The famous gardens are far below and the ledge beneath my feet barely wide enough for my boot, but this isn't my first time in a precarious position.

Just not when I'm half-drugged with Night's Bloom.

I can see the balcony that juts out from the prince's chambers. Ignoring the drop, I slip along the ledge like a cat and leap onto the balcony. I nearly miss the landing, muscles straining as I misjudge it. Muscle memory saves the day, and somehow I hook my leg over the balcony, even as the stone tiles loom far below.

Cauldron's piss, that was close. Sweat drips down my spine as I take a second to catch my breath. I swear I am going to wring my bloody sister's neck when I get my hands on her.

Hauling myself over the edge of the balcony, I crouch behind the gauzy curtains, knees trembling.

The sight that greets me shakes me to the core.

A woman straddles the prince, the violet sweep of her skirts—*my* skirts—sliding up her bare thigh.

A woman wearing my face.

The arts of glamour are gifted to all fae. You can't entirely change your appearance, but you can embellish it.

And Soraya and I look similar enough that one could almost be forgiven for the mistake, even without the heavy lashing of glamour she's applied.

Keir kisses his way up Soraya's throat, hands sliding up the silk covering her back as she arches her head back in a simulation of pleasure. Or, at least, what I hope is a fucking simulation. Because someone is moaning, and it damned well better not be her.

Then her hand slides into her skirts, lantern light glinting off the flash of a golden hilt strapped to her thigh.

And I am done.

Night's Bloom or no Night's Bloom, rage ignites within me, like a starved furnace granted oxygen.

I offered her a truce. But once again she's spat in my face.

And whatever I might have begun to feel for the prince —forbidden or not, hopeless or not—she has no right to try and take that from me.

Twisting through the shadows, I slam onto the bed, sending her sprawling off him. Half-shadow, half-flesh, I draw back my fist and punch her right in the mouth as she screams.

The knife makes a loud clatter as it hits the floor, but my rage knows nothing else.

Soraya grabs for my throat, but we're both scrambling for balance on the treacherous bed. Silk fucking sheets slither like snakes beneath us. I can't get a decent grip on her, but neither can she. We both hit the floor as a snarl erupts behind us, and suddenly I lose my grip on the Sift.

The shadows drain from the room around me as I physically manifest, rolling across the cold, marble tiles.

Keir's on his hands and knees, the glints of gold in his eye practically spitting sparks. And then he sees both of us facing each other and freezes. "What in the Cauldron's name is going on?"

I watch as his gaze locks on the discarded dagger. The claw that hung around his neck is beside it, as if she ripped it from his throat when I slammed into her. It's as if the veil is swept from his eyes. No more confusion. He understands *this*.

And curse it all, I can hear his voice speaking of trust. Of betrayal.

"Sorry, Your Highness," I gasp, as Soraya gives a vicious scream and launches at me. "Family dispute."

I block her blow. And then the second. Rage glints like a trapped predator in her eyes as she realizes I'm not the girl I was.

"Do you know," I taunt, "I've never really wanted to hit you until now."

"And yet you still haven't managed to strike a blow."

Oh, that does it.

I launch forward.

We're a whirlwind of elbows and knees. Enough poison must have hit my system, for it's harder to breathe now. Harder to block the next punch. Heaviness seeps through my limbs, and the rage that fueled me is dying.

And then something smashes us apart, like a fist of pure air slamming into my ribs.

I hit the floor, hands and legs flying, tumbling head over heels until I hit the wall.

Ow.

It's so tempting to stay down, to give in.

But an icy wind sweeps through the chamber, bringing with it an air of menace. And suddenly I'm reminded of the true predator in the room.

"*Enough.*" Prince Keir's golden skin glows internally, as if his body simply can't contain the magic radiating through him.

He makes a claw gesture with his hand, and a pair of glowing golden cuffs spring into being around my wrists.

I take one look at Soraya as similar cuffs snap around her wrists. Her lip curls in fury.

"Would love to stay, Your Highness." I push to my feet,

reaching for the shadows. "But I think it's time to put this farce to an end. You chose me before you knew what I was, but it's better it ends this way." My voice softens. "Now no one will get hurt. Goodbye."

I hurl myself into the shadows—

Only to flicker back into being as something stops me from melding with them. Slamming back into my physical body is an agony I never expected, and I find myself gasping on the floor.

"Don't deny your charms," the prince growls out. "I've never been more *intrigued* by you."

Soraya is gone.

And with her, the Dragon's Heart.

I slap my palm to the floor. Merciless bitch must have had a turnkey portal on her somewhere. Which means I'm the sole recipient of the prince's hot-eyed stare. Damn it.

She won again.

12

The golden cuffs around my wrists bite against my skin.

Or more precisely, the magic within me.

It's a horrible sensation, somewhat akin to being dumped in a swamp absolutely teeming with midges, and try as I might, I can't Sift.

"Are you done?" asks a cool, demanding voice.

Slumping against the chair I'm bound to, I look up at the speaker.

Prince Keir paces in front of me, and he looks *furious*. If he had a tail, I'm fairly certain it would be lashing behind him.

"Nice chains." I shrug. "Chair's a bit hard though."

His golden eyes narrow to thin slits. There's no more pretense of hazel in them, and it makes me a little nervous, for he no longer looks entirely fae. It's like the glamour he wields can't quite hide what's stretching beneath his skin.

And whatever it is, it looks like a predator.

"You'd prefer it if I tied you to the bed?"

I glance at the mess of silk sheets and the knife still lying on the floor. A shiver runs through me. "No. No. Chair is fine."

"Good choice." This time his voice drops several octaves, practically humming with power. He lashes out with his fingers, and half a dozen rips suddenly appear in the sheets. "I dislike being played for a fool. Who are you?" he demands, in a silky, dangerous tone of voice. "Because I'm fairly certain you're *not* Merisel of Greenslieves."

Excellent guess, Your Highness.

"Not quite."

"And that was your... sister?"

Who has left me to the prince's mercy without a backward glance. "One would think we owned such familial ties, but I believe I got the lion's share of all the best traits."

"Honesty?" he purrs. "Loyalty? Compassion?"

"I did try to warn you."

If anything the words only seem to make him angrier.

"Is this a good time to remind you that I *did* just save your life?"

"Perhaps you'd be wiser to keep your damned mouth shut," Keir growls. "Considering your sister just tried to put her knife in my heart."

"Well, if you hadn't had your tongue halfway down her throat, I daresay she wouldn't have gotten close enough to try."

He pauses, looking momentarily interested in the bite in my tone. "Jealous?"

"Very." I snort. "Why wouldn't I want a male who's fool enough to fall for a simple glamour and a few pretty words, no doubt?"

His eyes narrow. "The low neckline might have had something to do with it. I was distracted. And her eyes were definitely saying yes. I thought you'd changed your mind."

"Even better. After everything I've said, you thought I'd finally fallen at your feet?"

There's a growl in his voice. "She was *very* convincing."

Males often want what they can't have. No doubt Soraya used it against him. A little resistance, and then she starts to soften. Starts to fall for his charms.

It's an old trick that's won me through many a locked door in the past. Show a man you simply can't resist him, and his ego does the rest.

I'm not sure why it bothers me so much.

Keir flips the blade and snatches it from the air. "Goblin-forged blade. I assume these runes down the steel mean it can cut through any ward?"

"Any ward," I say with a sigh. "Any armor. Any flesh."

"So she meant to kill me."

Admitting it will probably not go well for me.

I press my lips together.

"Ah, you think you can hold out. I can wait for the truth," he purrs, grabbing another chair and hauling it in front of me. He straddles it backward, resting his forearms on the chair back. "It won't take long for those cuffs to eat their way through your glamour. You can already feel it, can't you?"

I shift uneasily. The itch is definitely getting stronger.

Is that...? Shit. There's a faint, luminous glow to my hands.

And I'm not the only one who's noticed.

"Interesting," says the Prince of Dreams.

Only, this time I'm convinced I'm in a nightmare.

"You glow," he muses. "Very few creatures glow. I think the truth of your nature is not so far away, after all. You could simply tell me. I might feel more merciful."

There's no love lost between the Blessed and the Forbidden. If he realizes what I am, he'll have my head on the next pike.

"What if I make a deal?" I blurt.

"A deal? Go on," he purrs. "What could you possibly give me that I can't take?"

"Information. You want your relic back? I can tell you everything."

"And in exchange?"

"You can't kill me. You can't harm me. You will forbid your men or anyone in or at the court from harming me."

"Or I could wait," he replies, eyeing the faint glow creeping up my arms. "It looks like it won't take long now."

Sweat trickles down my spine. "I could get the Dragon's Heart back for you."

At this he pauses. His eyes meet mine. "What makes you think I can't get it back myself?"

"Because if you do so, it means war. You'll be challenging a dangerous court. A powerful king."

"Will I?" There's a distinct lack of concern in his voice. "It wouldn't be the first time. And it won't be the last, no doubt."

There has to be something he wants.

"A king," he muses. "There are very few kings in the realm. And few with the balls to challenge me. King Angmar is currently underwhelming. Something about a missing trident, according to his dear sister, Ismena. He needs this match, so he won't risk a direct confrontation. King Jor is tied to the seas. King Mordred might be ambitious enough, but he's crossed me before. The King of the Unblessed hasn't been seen in centuries. And every other king is controlled by a queen."

Do not *react.*

"But there's one king I'm forgetting, isn't there? The King of the Frozen North. The King Beyond the Shadowfangs.

The Master of Bone and Death. They say wraiths glow in the night." He eyes my arms.

"They say they are monsters, too. What monster could hide itself in fae flesh?" I can't control the bitterness in my voice.

"That is the question." He flips the knife expertly in his fingers. "So the Wraith King sends a pair of assassins to my court."

"I'm *not* an assassin."

"No?"

I clamp my teeth shut.

His eyes narrow. "A thief then. And considering your sister stole the pretty charm around my throat, I assume you were after that."

"Shouldn't you be going after my sister?" I ask in exasperation. "*She's* the one who stole your relic, and with every second that passes she'll be getting closer to escaping for good!"

"The portal's closed. It has been ever since you arrived." Muscle flexes in his powerful forearms as he leans closer, the chair tipping onto two legs. "The only way anyone gets in or out... is if I let them."

"You don't know my sister. She has a turnkey portal she stole from a blood-witch years ago. She'll be able to steal her way home, without having to use your portal. How do you think she got out of this room?"

"How did *you* get in? You appeared out of nowhere."

"Magic," I whisper.

Keir eases out of the chair, his bare feet padding toward me. Every inch of me is alight. There's no hiding it as he tips my chin up, the knife still curled in his left hand. "A very rare, ancient magic I haven't seen in thousands of years. I knew a male once who could walk the shadows." He tips my face from side to side. "And yet you glow with the Forbidden's curse. An intriguing conundrum, for you're far too pretty to be wraith-born, yet you're not entirely fae, are you?"

"Why the fascination with me?" I snap. "You might have paid me lip service in the past, but don't pretend it was more than that."

"When you simpered and flattered me and skirted the truth like a court princess sweeping her train out of a pile of vomit?"

"Sorry," I drawl. "I was trying *not* to capture your attention."

"You nearly succeeded." His golden eyes are strangely cloaked. I can't read the expression on his face. "But you did. I would have made you my mate."

I close my eyes. "I think you wanted to be fooled."

"And I think the only time you weren't lying to me was when you told me you liked me."

"It was just a ploy." I make a sound of exasperation, because it's better than letting the conversation venture into such dangerous waters. "Anyone would think you didn't give a damn that you just lost a powerful relic."

"But did I?" His smile turns dangerous. "What makes you think your sister managed to steal the real Dragon's Heart?"

My gaze jerks to his. "What do you mean?"

"The real Dragon's Heart has the power to create an Other World. The power to destroy the real world. Do you not think I would have given chase if what she stole was more than mere gold?"

"It wasn't in the treasury."

"No." Again, another smile. His eyes seem to glow from within. "Nor hanging around my neck. Guess again, little thief."

Calliope's words bite through me again. Her absolute insistence she needed to eat the prince's heart to transform.

I'd thought her mad.

I'd thought her stories were just that.

But it suddenly occurs to me: What is the best place to hide a relic of such immense power?

You twist the tale. Change the story. The *Dragon's Heart*. It's been right there in front of me the entire time.

Nobody knows what truly happened to the dragons—the stories are lost to history—but I know they slowly faded from the world. Some say they turned to stone, some say they sought the stars, and some say....

"What are *you*?" I whisper.

Again, a faint mocking smile. "You're not the one asking the questions."

But his eyes glint gold—dragon gold—and I can't help remembering the other part of the stories. Dragons are invulnerable. Nobody knows how the ancient fae defeated them.

But what if the stories lie?

What if there *was* no defeat?

What if Calliope was telling the truth?

My gaze slips to his open shirt and the hard planes of his chest. He admitted he created this Other World himself, and I assumed he used the relic to do it, but if I'm right, then he would have the power of such creation at his fingertips.

Mother of Mercy.

I try to scramble backward and the chair scrapes on the tiles, but Keir merely clenches his fist.

My chair squeals as I'm hauled directly in front of him.

Keir grabs me by the wrists, his long fingers locking around the cuffs there. Heat spills through me as his magic slides across my skin like a caress. "I've heard what you've had to say. Now it's my turn. You owe me. I will offer *you* a deal. Your life, your freedom, in exchange for a year and a day of service."

Service? It sounds like a trap. "What do you want me to do?"

"Something similar to what you do now. I may ask you to fetch me something. I may ask for information. I may ask you to betray your precious king. And when I do, you'll give it to me."

"I won't kill for you."

"Agreed."

"And you won't hurt me? You won't allow me to *be* hurt?"

His eyes seem shadowed in thought. "Not by me or mine. I cannot stop someone else from putting an arrow through your back."

It's the best I'm going to get.

I consider the cuffs.

A year and a day of service, as according to the old laws. In return, my head remains on my shoulders. I've been offered worse terms before.

"I'm not saying no," I mutter. "But there's a slight compli-cation. I owe a similar debt to the Wraith King. I can't deny him outright."

"I'm not certain this is my problem."

Of course not. Typical fae prince. "Then I'm dead and of no use to you."

Our gazes lock.

He considers it. "Then I will allow you to work around the debt you owe your king."

"Agreed," I whisper.

The cuffs fall free.

I'm halfway to my feet before I realize there's no escape. Keir looms in front of me, shadows darkening half of his face. I force my feet to still, even though my body quivers as I fight my natural instincts.

But there's no point running.

He never confirmed it, but he rules this world with a thought. He could crush me with a single swat of his hand.

Besides, I have nowhere to run.

I can outthink this. I can escape. All I need is a little time.

Capturing my face in both hands, he tilts my chin up.

"A year and day of service," he whispers, and then lowers his face to mine.

The kiss breathes across my lips, and I can feel his magic stealing through me. My heart suddenly flutters like a horde of butterflies set loose inside me, a restless, liquid heat stealing through my veins, and setting me ablaze. He kisses as if he means to consume me, but the bite of his magic leaves the taste of blood in my mouth.

And suddenly it's no longer pleasurable.

Fire blazes beneath my skin, a searing kind of magic that steals every thought from my mind. A scream escapes me as it brands itself up my arms, golden light spilling through sudden glyphs that appear on my skin. I don't need to count them. I can feel them igniting inside me. All four hundred and thirteen marks.

A year and a day.

By the time it's done, I'm shaking in his arms, my knees boneless and my fists curled in his shirt.

And worse. I can feel his heart pounding beneath my hand, beating in sync with mine.

"What d-did you do to me?"

"I have marked you as my own. There is no escape now." He doesn't have to sound so thrilled about it. "You belong to me, my little thief," he purrs. "Mind you don't forget it."

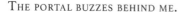

THE PORTAL BUZZES BEHIND ME.

Freedom's so close I can almost taste it, and yet it remains a taunt. The golden glyphs on my arms have faded, but I can still feel them settled beneath my skin, as if tattooed into my very bones.

Within seconds, I'll be back in my own world.

Back within my father's grasp and under his command.

But this time, I'm at the mercy of another male, and Keir's forbidden me to tell anyone of the deal we made.

I'm getting rather tired of being someone else's pawn. But for now, there's little choice in the matter.

"Go home, little thief." Keir looms in front of me, dressed in a doublet of black velvet that caresses the hard planes of his chest. He sets the tip of a finger beneath my chin, forcing me to meet his eyes. "Say nothing of what occurred here. When I have a task for you, I'll contact you."

"How?"

He smiles. "You'll know."

"What do I tell the king?" Soraya will have beaten me home, and he'll hear this tale from her lips first.

"I'm sure you'll think of something. Let us not pretend you're averse to lies."

The glyphs on my arms pulse as if he's stroked his finger down my skin. I can't help a shiver.

I step through the waterfall and stare over the stone ledge into the circular well as thousands of pounds of water sluice down its sides. Mist curls up through its hollow core, but far below, I catch the golden gleam of glyphs that herald a portal.

"How do I get through the portal?" I call, teeth gritted against the chill as water splashes me.

"Jump," Prince Keir suggests.

Oh, yes. He's still angry. I miss the tender way he touched my face. The way he kissed my forehead as if I were precious.

But I always knew it would end this way.

Closing my eyes, I step onto the ledge.

Somehow I don't feel safe.

I feel like I've just made a deal with the dragon itself.

But the only choice I have is to trust him.

And jump.

~

BEFORE YOU LEAVE THE COURT OF DREAMS WORLD

Dear Reader,

Thank you so much for reading! If you enjoyed *Thief of Dreams*, then keep an eye out for the *Thief of Souls* release!

After failing to return with the Dragon's Heart, Zemira is

sent by her father to infiltrate the Court of Blood, in search of the mythical cauldron that contains the power of the long-lost dragon kings.

But her deal with Prince Keir bears dangerous consequences—for Keir is determined to gain the cauldron himself. Caught between two deadly enemies, can Zemira save herself? And will Keir ever forgive her for the deception she played upon him?

Make sure you sign up to my newsletter to be the first to know when *Thief of Souls* is available.

Here are some other ways to stay updated:
* Follow me on Bookbub
* Visit my website at becmcmaster.com
*Or join my Facebook Fan Group for all the exclusive stuff!

I hope we meet again between the pages of another book!

Cheers,
Bec McMaster

P.S Want more fantasy romance? Read on for a preview of **Promise of Darkness**, *a fairy tale twist on the Hades and Persephone myth.*

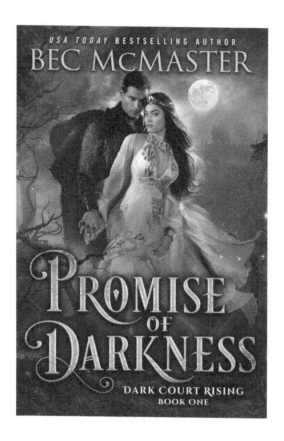

Princess. Tribute. Sacrifice. Is she the one prophesied to unite two warring Fae courts? Or the one bound to destroy them?

In a realm ruled by magi

c, the ruthless Queen of Thorns is determined to destroy her nemesis, the cursed Prince of Evernight.

With war brewing between the bitter enemies, the prince forces Queen Adaia to uphold an ancient treaty: she will send one of her daughters to his court as a political hostage for three months.

The queen insists it's the perfect opportunity for Princess Iskvien to end the war before it begins. But one look into Thiago's smouldering eyes and Vi knows she's no assassin.

The more secrets she uncovers about the prince and his court, the more she begins to question her mother's motives.

Who is the true enemy? The dark prince who threatens her heart? Or the ruthless queen who will stop at nothing to destroy him?

And when the curse threatens to shatter both courts, is she strong enough to break it?

A fairytale twist inspired by the Hades and Persephone myth.

READ NOW

EXCERPT

Two dresses hang in the closet in front of me, both gauzy and overflowing with far too much fabric. Neither are my preferred style, but that's not the point.

Tonight is Lammastide and appearances have to be met.

Tonight I'm not Iskvien, second daughter of a merciless queen. Tonight I'm an Asturian princess, ruthless in her own right, invulnerable to those who might seek to bring down my mother's court. It might only be silk, but it's armor of a kind, though I'd far prefer a chain mail vest.

"Wear the red," says a clipped voice from the doorway. "It will accentuate your dark hair and olive skin."

My fingers still on the fabric. "Mother. What a pleasant surprise."

It is neither.

She wasn't here when we returned from the hunt. It's been three days. And I know my sister, Andraste, made her report.

I've been waiting for the queen to make an appearance, and point out all the ways in which I fail her. Queen Adaia is not the type to strike immediately. She likes to let her opponents wait. And each day she hesitates is one more hint of her displeasure, one more sign it's going to be fatal.

Three days.... Not quite a storm of rage that could threaten to tear the palace apart, but a quiet, deadly chill, I suspect. Like the breath of winter down your spine.

I turn as the queen sweeps inside the room, her heavy silver gown dragging over the marble tiles with a rasp. We're as different as night and day, and I see Andraste in the queen's features, which is simply another reminder of whom the favorite daughter is. They share the same stubborn chin and full mouth, high-swept cheekbones highlighting the vaguely feline shape of their blue eyes.

But Mother's hair is wheaten gold, drawn up into a coronet of braids upon which rests her sharp-pointed crown. And she's taller, slightly thinner. More dangerous.

Anyone looking at the two of us might wonder if we shared any blood at all.

"To what do I owe this pleasure, Mother?" It's the edge of impertinence, which is all she will allow. "Won't we be late to the Queensmoot?"

"They'll wait."

"You expect an attack?" Lammastide is the one night of the year when all five surviving kingdoms of the Seelie Alliance come together to bring in the new year. Drinking, dancing, bloodshed, and assassinations are all to be expected.

Because allied we may be, but it's only against a common enemy. If my mother could destroy the other rulers of the alliance, she wouldn't hesitate.

In some part of her mind, she sees herself sitting on a throne that rules over the entire southern half of the continent.

"Sit," she says.

The only option is to obey.

"No attack." She slinks behind me as I take a seat at the vanity. "Or nothing beyond the usual. The Prince of Evernight will be there, after all. He craves my downfall."

Someone's projecting.

"I thought the Unseelie delegation would be the greater danger?"

Five hundred years ago we defeated them in the Wars of Light and Shadow, but the peace has always been tenuous. This recent treaty between Seelie and Unseelie courts is a relatively new development, and if I were my mother's daughter, I wouldn't trust it.

The three witch queens of the Unseelie court are bloodthirsty, vicious, and powerful. If my mother has delusions of grandeur, then they're nothing compared to the Unseelie, who want to cast us all into chains.

The queen lifts the heavy strands of my hair from my shoulders and runs her jeweled claws through it. "Queen Angharad is still bleeding from that last skirmish, and some say she doesn't have the full support of her sister queens any more. She's trying to fight a war on two fronts, so she won't have the courage to cause trouble for us. Focus on the real danger, Iskvien. Those at your back. Those with a knife to your throat." Her claws caress my collarbone. "Those who were never meant to rule the earth beneath their feet."

She's speaking of the two Seelie princes who forced their way onto the thrones of their own kingdoms. The Seelie kingdoms have been matrilineal for centuries—queens are tied to the lands, and the earth beneath them flourishes from the bond. Any kings that sought to elevate themselves were slowly and mercilessly destroyed. My mother considers Prince Thiago and Prince Kyrian's claims to be unnatural, and she's been working on ruining them ever since they proclaimed themselves.

Prince Kyrian never attends the Lammastide rites in person. Mother once mocked him for the loss of the woman he loved, and he swore an oath that if he ever set eyes upon her again, he'd have her head. To uphold the peace, he sends an envoy to the rites in his stead.

So she's talking of Evernight.

Always Evernight.

My thoughts stray to the forest and the bane. The creature who knew me.

And the Prince of Evernight, who rules the dark kingdom.

"What should I expect?" I've never met the prince. These are the first Lammastide rites my mother's allowed me to attend. "Will the Prince of Evernight avoid us?"

"Unfortunately, not. He considers me responsible for the loss of his wife, and I daresay he's still determined to have his revenge upon me. In fact, he's the reason I'm here."

Here it is. I still, like prey catching scent of a dangerous predator as she moves to the side, considering the array of scents and powders on my vanity.

"What does he have to do with me?"

"You're not coming home with us tonight, Iskvien," my mother says, lifting the stopper of my perfume vial and sniffing delicately at the scent within. Her nose wrinkles.

I blink.

"*What?*"

"The Prince of Evernight agreed to a truce over the territories of Mistmere after that unfortunate clash near the border, but it has come at a price."

I feel the edges of the world sucking at me. "What price?"

"There are to be hostages, to prove our good faith. His cousin is to be exchanged tonight, for you."

The jaws of the trap spring shut. I shouldn't have trusted her sweet smile, her gentle touch.

"You bartered me away? Like a fucking trinket?"

The queen's eyes narrow. "Watch your tone, daughter."

Rage fills me, but it's tempered with the quicksilver flash of fear. All these years I've been wary of her temper, but this is.... How do I...?

"It's only for three months," she continues, as if I've accepted it.

The prince could do anything to me in the space of three months. If he thinks my mother killed his wife, then I daresay I'm to be a proxy for his vengeance.

"Is this punishment?" The words erupt from my mouth. "For failing to kill that bane? It was just a hesitation, Mother. Andraste stole the kill. It won't happen again."

"*What* hesitation?"

Andraste didn't tell her?

The queen's face tightens imperceptibly, and her hands come to rest upon my shoulders. The tip of each of her fingers is covered in a silver claw, the points pressing into my collarbone. Thin chains connect them to the gauntlets around her wrist. It's nothing more than a focus for her powers—not that many know that—but the effect is also eerily threatening.

She doesn't say a word.

She doesn't have to.

"Andraste was faster than I," I say swiftly, to cover my misstep. "I thought she'd told you."

"The bane is of little consequence."

I square my shoulders. "Why worry about a ferocious beast when you're throwing me to the wolves?"

"You are not to be harmed."

"Of course not. Am I to be his whore instead?"

She arches a brow at my tone. "You are to be his political hostage, Iskvien. Make whatever bargains you need to, to keep yourself safe. But remember…, his cousin will be in my hands."

And any harm that befalls me will be returned in kind.

"Forgive me, Mother, if such a concept brings me little peace. They say the prince betrayed his queen and murdered her sons. I daresay he'll not hesitate to consider his cousin to be an acceptable loss if he can strike a blow upon you."

"You disappoint me, daughter. I offer you an opportunity, and you throw it in my face."

This is another one of her challenges. *Prove yourself*, she's telling me. *Show me you have the strength and wit to survive.*

"What opportunity?"

"There is a way you could serve your queen while you

are there." My mother unsheathes the dagger at her belt and places it on the vanity in front of me.

Star-forged steel. No trueborn fae can wield the iron that lies on this world, but this knife was forged from the heart of a fallen comet, and its iron came from beyond the stars.

As long as I don't touch the blade itself, I can use it.

For a second, I see his blood splashed across the marble tiles of his palace, the knife planted between his shoulder blades. An end to the monstrous lord of the Evernight court, and freedom for those Asturians who've been imprisoned in the war camps. No more fighting. No more endless wars. No more scheming and politicking.

But murder, just the same.

"No," I say abruptly. "I'm no assassin."

Adaia leans down, her face resting on my shoulder and her gaze meeting mine in the mirror. "Perhaps not. But he'd never expect it. Not from you, with your soft heart and those pretty eyes. And perhaps you should consider your people. The Kingdom of Asturia has been at war with Evernight for centuries. Whilst this treaty sparks a fragile truce, it doesn't mean anything. We could end this war with a single strike. We would own Mistmere, perhaps more...."

I push away from her, the hem of my silk wrap brushing against my calves. "Murder, Mother. I'm the first person they'll point the finger at. Who do you think they'll blame? If I kill the prince, then his people will execute me immediately, and their armies will rise against you."

"Not if it's self-defense," she points out.

So now I'm to frame an assassination as an assault by the prince.

"Thiago has no heir," she continues. "Without him, his generals will fight for control of his armies. It will be chaos, and I will crush them."

I notice she doesn't address the part where I lose my head.

"Take the dagger."

It's not a suggestion.

I pick it up, feeling the weight of it. Accepting it doesn't mean I have to go through with anything.

"I'll consider it." I catch a glimpse of my mother's dangerous smile in the reflection as the queen backs away. It wouldn't surprise me if she made this bargain with this end in mind.

"You have an hour. Get dressed and meet us in the courtyard. We ride for the Hallow. Wear the red."

Then she's gone.

Leaving me trembling.

I can't believe she gave me no warning. Or maybe that was deliberate: With a hint of what was to come, I might have been able to flee or outmaneuver this treaty. Now, I don't have a choice. The stamp of the guard's feet as they settle outside my door is jarringly loud, and my mother expects me in the courtyard within an hour.

This isn't merely hesitating to strike a killing blow against a monster.

This is politics, and she will brook no refusal.

But who would I rather face? My mother or a volatile, dangerous prince who might think me a plaything?

My resolve firms. If he thinks he's getting a trinket to toy with, then he had best think again.

The prince of the Kingdom of Evernight is Unseelie to his bones, despite the fact he claims to be Seelie. I can't afford to show him even a hint of my weak underbelly.

And curse my mother, but I'll be damned to the Underworld if I'll let her think me her puppet.

I fling the wardrobe open, both the red and the white

gowns tumbling in a frothy mess to the floor. Inside the wardrobe, right at the back, is *the* dress.

It's like a piece of pure midnight was carved from the sky, diamond stars glittering down its silken length. I don't know what urged me to have it made. Mother's right: vibrant colors suit me best. And yet, I'd been unable to think of anything else the moment I saw the material.

Red would be a sign of groveling.

The white is probably what she intended me to wear all along.

But this.... Time to show her I refuse to bow to her whims. This princess has claws. And she's not afraid to use them.

CONTINUE READING

ALSO BY BEC MCMASTER

DARK COURT RISING

Promise of Darkness

Crown of Darkness (coming 2020)

Curse of Darkness (coming 2021)

LEGENDS OF THE STORM SERIES

Heart Of Fire

Storm of Desire

Clash of Storms

Storm of Fury (coming 2019)

COURT OF DREAMS SAGA

Thief of Dreams

Thief of Shadows (coming)

Thief of Souls (coming)

LONDON STEAMPUNK SERIES

Kiss Of Steel

Heart Of Iron

My Lady Quicksilver

Forged By Desire

Of Silk And Steam

Novellas in same series:

Tarnished Knight

The Clockwork Menace

LONDON STEAMPUNK: THE BLUE BLOOD CONSPIRACY

Mission: Improper

The Mech Who Loved Me

You Only Love Twice

To Catch A Rogue

Dukes Are Forever

DARK ARTS SERIES

Shadowbound

Hexbound

Soulbound

BURNED LANDS SERIES

Nobody's Hero

The Last True Hero

The Hero Within

SHORT STORIES

The Many Lives Of Hadley Monroe

Burn Bright

ABOUT THE AUTHOR

BEC MCMASTER is a writer, a dreamer, and a travel addict. If she's not sitting in front of the computer, she's probably plotting her next overseas trip, and hopes to see the whole world, whether it's by paper, plane, or imagination.

Bec grew up on a steady diet of '80s fantasy movies like *Ladyhawke*, *Labyrinth*, and *The Princess Bride*, and loves creating epic, fantasy-based romances with heroes and heroines who must defeat all the odds to have their HEA. She lives in Australia with her very own hero, where she can be found creating fantasy-fueled worlds, where even the darkest hero can find love.

Read more at <u>www.becmcmaster.com</u>

Made in the USA
Monee, IL
02 December 2020